A QUESTION OF SURVIVAL

by

Alice K. Arenz

DEDICATION

For Linda & Bill, and the vacation that started it all

AUTHOR'S NOTE & ACKNOWLEDGEMENTS

It's been over forty years since the seed of this book was planted by a trip with family and friends into the backcountry of the Colorado Rockies. After pounding out the first version of the manuscript on a typewriter, followed by eight computers, I often wondered if Jessica's story would ever be completed. Who knew it would take a pandemic to finally make that happen? God did.

I'd like to thank my wonderful editor, awesome publisher, extended family, friends, and tolerant husband—the last of which heard "just let me run one more thing by you," far more times than can be counted. I love you all!

Thank you, Father, for waiting for me to listen to that still, small voice, and for showing me the way.

aka

He knew exactly how to hurt me so it wouldn't leave any marks—at least on the outside. Would I ever be capable of doing the same to him?

I asked myself that question every time he abused me. It didn't matter whether it was through careless words or deeds... or with his hands. Oh, the hands stung more, but the words stayed with me long after the redness of the slap or the bruises faded away. The comments were like barbed wire poking and sticking me, a constant reminder of all the ways I could never measure up to his level of perfection.

The rhythmic tick of the ceiling fan and clicking of the pull chain from each revolution pierced my brain in much the same way as the harsh hundred-watt bulbs in the light—all things to *his* specifications.

Too much illumination, too much sound, too many thoughts, too many emotions...

Huddling in the corner where I'd sought solace, Domino, my one true companion, inched forward on her belly. Even my little dog knew to fly under the radar when Jonathan was in one of these moods. Something that happened more and more frequently.

Domino crept onto my lap and whimpered. It was a soft cry, barely audible, something only we could hear—a cry from the heart between the two of us.

I hugged her to me, holding back tears that threatened to fall. Jonathan hated when I cried. Since it would only make him angry and more disagreeable, what was the use?

Burying my face into her soft fur, I thanked God for my little dog and her companionship. I'd never been allowed a pet, wasn't allowed friends that weren't preapproved by Jonathan. But even he couldn't dismiss a gift from my formidable grandmother.

Drawing a deep breath, I peered around the dresser and wished for a way to be absorbed into the wall behind me. A nice thought, but imagination didn't count when dealing with Jonathan. Once you were in his reality, that's where you remained.

He'd gone into the bathroom to shower after the… encounter. He'd expect me to be ready by the time he was finished.

I set my trembling dog on the floor and struggled to stand. My ribs hurt, but a quick examination with practiced fingers told me nothing was cracked. That was good. Having to drive to an emergency room in another town was not on tonight's agenda.

The dress he expected me to wear dangled over the side of the bed where he'd tossed it, the one thing in the orderly room that was more out of place than me. I fingered the red and black material, my teeth gritting from the strange combination of threads that were soft in appearance yet scratchy to wear. He knew how much it bothered me, how uncomfortable I would be. He didn't care. It was my punishment for wanting to avoid the party.

Not a party. My mother didn't throw parties; she arranged get-togethers—and always with just the right people.

None of which interested me.

Except Daddy.

Thinking about my father brought the tears I'd kept from shedding during and after Jonathan's—chastisement. Daddy was a dear, sweet man whose main goal in life was to do his best to help others in any way he could. He never saw the world for what it truly was, only saw the good that existed and what things could be with a little assistance. It explained why he'd never *really seen* Jonathan and my mother.

Or my brother.

After swiping away the tears, I tore off my jeans and t-shirt and threw on the dress. My drawers were in such a state of disarray, I almost didn't find the one good pair of pantyhose I possessed. I'd have to get the dresser tidied up before Jonathan decided to do a spot inspection.

"I'm nearly finished, Jessica." The deep baritone of his voice boomed through the closed bathroom door as I hastened to slip into the hose. "How are you doing?"

"I-I'll just need to fix my hair and makeup when you're out." I cringed in preparation for the reprisal I was sure would come and was surprised when it didn't happen.

Jonathan pulled open the door and strode into the room. As usual, he was impeccably groomed with every hair in place. His sporty, button-down shirt and casual slacks crisp, carefully ironed to his standard of perfection. I'd never known anyone who worked so hard to appear relaxed and laid back.

"You look great." I said, sliding past him into the bathroom.

He didn't respond; he didn't have to. My comment was simply a mandated response. Another in a long list of things learned from his iron will to prove I gave him the deference he deserved.

One glance in the mirror told me I was in for more trouble. My long, curly hair was as out of control as the frightened look in my eyes. I had about ten minutes to tame them both.

"Wear it up tonight, Jess."

He stood in the doorway watching as I tugged the brush through the unruly mass. I didn't turn from the mirror, just gave him a weak smile; something I hoped he wouldn't notice. As I reached for a hair band, he came up behind me and put his hands on my shoulders.

Don't flinch, don't react. Just give in and pretend as you always do. The words repeated themselves in my mind as his lips caressed the back of my neck while I pulled my hair into a ponytail.

I continued to work on my hair, knowing that a reaction—any reaction—was likely to bring on another tirade.

"There's a good girl, Jess." Jonathan said, running his hands down my sides, across my chest, to finally roam all over my body. "You're doing just fine, little girl. Just fine."

Don't feel the hands. Don't feel…

Dear God make me numb, please make me numb!

These false caresses were far more dangerous than his open-handed slaps or fists. But I knew my place, knew what was expected of, and from, me.

I reached deep inside for anything that could take me out of the present into an alternate reality, sliding on a mask I hoped would hide my true feelings, all while pinning my hair into a bun then touching up mascara and blush.

Pain, not pleasure. Degradation not glorification. These were part and parcel to Jonathan's pseudo tenderness. It was all about him, all about what he wanted and desired. Opposing him was out of the question.

Just as reminding him I was not supposed to engage in sexual activity.

Intense discomfort shot through me, riveting me to the spot and halting any further progress on my makeup. I held onto the edge of the countertop, closed my eyes and resumed my prayers, those fervent utterances begging for release… to be turned to stone.

He was finished before I was able to regain any semblance of composure. He didn't appear to notice. When he turned away and walked across the room to his sink, I tried to breathe, to collect myself, and realized I'd been holding my breath. As air rushed into my lungs, a stifled sound escaped, bringing Jonathan's eyes up to his mirror. His sneer flashed from one mirror to the other.

Without a word he put me in my place, demoting me to something below the rank of human being.

I was given no extra time, no chance to clean myself up, add a touch of cologne, or anything else. When Jonathan was ready to leave, I was expected to be ready as well.

His will, not mine.

When will it be my will, God? *When will it be Yours?*

Chapter 2

The car seat felt cold and hard, difficult to sit on after what just happened. When my squirming caught Jonathan's eye, he flashed me a disapproving glare. It was enough to bring me back into submission and keep me still.

I gazed out the windshield, focusing on the road and the fog that crept up the corners of the window. As it inched its way onto the glass, Jonathan released an exasperated sigh and switched on the defroster. He didn't like using the heat if it wasn't absolutely necessary. Trying to regulate the temperature inside the car with the outside always tried his patience. Too much heat, even if necessary to keep the windshield clear, would make him sweat, and that was unacceptable.

Jonathan's ambitions ranked far above anything else in his life. His education and limited resources had kept him out of the one arena in which he'd always wanted to be a big player: politics. Knowing he would never make it in the circles where money talked and ability was secondary to charm and charisma, he'd returned to the small community where he'd grown up. Once here, he'd set his sights on infiltrating the only political game in town, centered on a reluctant mayor and his ambitious wife—my parents. After gaining my mother's confidence and support, he set his sights on me. And once he'd done so, *my* life was no longer my own.

As we pulled onto my parents' street, Jonathan cleared his throat and tightened his hands on the steering wheel.

"None of your remarks about the "timeliness" of this party. You're to smile and be friendly whether you want to or not. There's bound to be discussion about what happened three days ago, but you keep it in perspective, do you understand? No going off on one of your tangents. They don't want to hear it any more than I do." He didn't wait for acknowledgement, just continued his instructions for my behavior. "And I don't want you harping on the miscarriage, either. This is a fundraiser for your father, not Jessica's pity party."

We pulled to a stop across the street from my childhood home. Every light in the place was on, giving the illusion of warmth and comfort. There were already so many people in attendance some had spilled onto the front lawn. This meant it was likely several more occupied the lawn chairs out back as well. The slight chill to the evening air wouldn't be felt after they'd had a few drinks. By then they wouldn't notice the persistence of my mother and her demand for cash in support of my father's campaign. Though why it was necessary to hold these fundraisers or even call it a campaign I never understood. There were never any serious candidates running against him.

Because there were people around to witness it, Jonathan opened my door and helped me out of the car. He draped an arm around my shoulders and deftly pinched the tender area between my breast and underarm. It was his way to subtly warn me to adhere to his list of do's and don'ts.

"—and he said if the bears don't get you, the wild dogs will!" Gavin Hardesty laughed loudly as he clapped another man across the back. Not only was he the owner of the largest car dealership in town, he was also my father's best friend.

"Here come the J's," Gavin announced, a broad smile plastered across his face. He gave me a welcoming hug. His wife, Mary, less gregarious but sweet and conciliatory, followed suit.

"How're you doing, honey?" Mary reached up and brushed my bangs from my forehead. "We were sorry to hear about the miscarriage."

Jonathan, who had regained control by taking hold of my elbow, squeezed it now. He didn't care for Gavin Hardesty and despised his overly familiar use of our initials.

"I'm fine, Mary. Thanks for asking." I smiled, hoping it reached my eyes and didn't betray my true emotions. It must have worked. Mary patted my cheek and then turned back to her husband who'd continued his former conversation.

"It could be coyotes, of course, but you know Yangston once he's onto something. Said there were wild dogs as rabid as wolves-"

My curiosity was piqued, and I would've liked to listen to this odd discussion, but Jonathan's cast-iron grip on my elbow prevented it. We continued into the house where he steered me to the dining room where the loudest group had gathered—a sure sign my mother was present.

Once there, he left my side for more intriguing company, that of a young woman with wavy red hair who was in the thick of the animated discussion. I vaguely recalled seeing her before but couldn't have said where. Likely at another of my mother's soirees.

When Jonathan joined the group, Mother lifted her head and glanced over to where I stood by the entrance to the room. Even after I'd become an adult, I remained in awe of her. She was tall and statuesque, not short like me, and the way she held herself always gave me the impression of royalty—a kind of do-not-touch superiority that left you wondering if you were worthy to be in her presence. Or maybe it was just my imagination working overtime like my brother once told me.

When she returned her attention to the group, I slipped away, hoping to find my father.

As I headed for the stairs, it felt like all the blood had been drained from my body. The sudden lightheadedness sent me crashing into the newel post. I clung to it as an out-of-body sensation washed over me. Pins and needles stabbed my hands and feet while the pain in my womb slashed downward, heightening the sensations of Jonathan's painful attack. Sounds whirred and buzzed around me, louder and louder until I was spinning out of control. I clung to the post, determined to ride it out, praying I wouldn't be noticed. Or worse, begin to scream.

When the dizziness passed, I took the opportunity to trudge up the stairs and into the bathroom which connected to my old bedroom. After closing the door, I grabbed a cup from the dispenser and shoved it under the tap, finally ready to try the medicine I'd been prescribed ten days ago.

The fall down the basement stairs hadn't just caused the miscarriage; it also banged me up so badly the doctor remarked it was a miracle I'd survived. I was still covered with black and blue marks. And the pain...

I spilled most of the first glass of water. The next glass washed down the Vicodin I was thankful to have stuffed into my purse before leaving the house. Perhaps the medicine could relieve the pain and take away the disgust I felt for my inability to protect the fragile life that had been inside me.

The label on the side of the container warned it could cause dizziness, against operating heavy machinery, and that alcohol could cause an adverse effect. Since I didn't plan on drinking, driving, or operating heavy machinery, there was nothing to worry about. Before replacing the cap, I downed another pill and then slid to the floor.

Why is it such a comfort to enfold oneself in your own arms? Does it trick the mind and body somehow and make it believe that someone else is holding you? Whatever the reason, I felt the comfort, the gentle touch that spoke of love and tenderness. Perhaps it wasn't my arms alone enfolding me in that cocoon of warmth. Maybe an angel, or God Himself, was on the floor with me. That's what I wanted to believe.

I closed my eyes and allowed my imagination to

run free. Rocking back and forth, back and forth, humming a song whose lyrics I didn't want to remember but offered comfort.

If only for a moment.

A tap on the door brought me rudely out of my idyll.

"Just a minute." I called.

Standing, I checked my face in the mirror over the sink. There was a little more color in my cheeks than there'd been a few minutes before, and, remarkably, the pain had already begun to subside.

I opened the door to find my best friend and former classmate waiting to use the facilities. I hadn't seen Claire Benton, now Lofgren, since her wedding three years ago, though not because I wanted it that way. Jonathan wasn't overly fond of Claire or her husband and always managed to find a reason for canceling outings with them whenever they were in Bennington. Still, we kept in contact via letters and the occasional phone conversation that lasted for hours. Calls that Claire instigated, of course. She still looked the same: pretty, perky, and peppy. And very pregnant.

"Jessie!" She threw her arms around me. "I was hoping to see you tonight. Now, you stay right there till I get out. I'll just be a sec."

When I nodded, my head seemed to bob in slow motion. I needed to sit down.

"I'll be in there," I pointed to my old room. "We can visit in private."

"Okey dokey. Be right out."

Claire disappeared inside the bathroom, and I headed straight for the bed. I sank onto the pristine white and gold spread that now covered it and wondered what my mother would think when she saw it had been wrinkled. Ordinarily I'd have worried. Right now, all I wanted was to lie down, pull that pompous looking bedspread over my head, and block out the world.

I sat on the edge of the bed, my feet remaining on the floor. It wasn't particularly comfortable, but would have to do.

With my eyes closed, the sound of the party took on a dull roar that slowly evaporated into nothing. I knew the horde was still there, but the cessation of immediate sound was so welcome that I bathed in it. There was no attempting to explain the feeling; I was in a heavenly vacuum for the moment, protected and calmed both inside and out.

"Ew, what has your mother done to your room?"

My eyes did a little jig when I opened them and found Claire studying my mother's attempt to turn my old bedroom into one of chic elegance. The white and gold creation was a far cry from the deep blues and warm reds which I'd loved.

"Your mother never breaks her stride, does she?" Claire shrugged her shoulders and joined me on the bed. She fingered the brocade spread and rolled her eyes. I laughed but didn't dare roll my eyes. I was afraid they'd pop out onto the floor. "I was, er, surprised when she didn't cancel this shindig after what happened, then remembered who I was thinking about." She wrinkled her nose. "And all the people here! It's just wrong somehow."

It only took a moment for me to remember this was Claire, a fellow conspirator and confidant, not someone who would criticize or judge me.

"I agree." I nodded, immediately regretting the action.

Claire grabbed my hand, giving it a gentle squeeze. "So, how are you doing, Cookie?"

I grinned at the use of the nickname she'd given me when we were small, and I'd chased her around the yard holding a bag of cookies she'd tried to swipe from me.

"I'd rather talk about this," I said, placing my hand on her enormous stomach. "I never thought you'd get out of a size two. Now look at you!"

Claire put her hand over mine while her other one brushed away a tear trickling down her cheek. It had been years since we'd really spent any time together, but the bond we shared as toddlers and all the way through school could never really be broken. I knew she was as upset about my miscarriage as I had been, just as she knew I didn't want to discuss it.

"The little devil has played havoc with my eating—which seems constant anymore. I've gained about thirty pounds, and with another eight weeks to go, I don't even want to think about how I'll look when he or she makes an appearance."

"So, you didn't find out the sex?"

Claire shook her head, her shiny dark hair dancing about her shoulders. "Nope. Tommy and I decided we wanted to do it the old-fashioned way." Her giggle reminded me of all the times we'd spent in this room sharing secrets and trying to figure out a way for my mother to like me as much as she liked Claire. We'd never come up with a solution.

"What about you, Cookie? What did the doctor say about you and Jonny-boy trying again?"

"Not a problem." That much was true. I didn't bother telling her that as much as I wanted a child there was no way I would bring one into the world while I was with Jonathan. And since he'd never allow a divorce, that meant not fulfilling the dream of motherhood.

"Terrific!" Claire clapped her hands then readjusted her position on the bed. "I want our kids to be best friends like we are. Or, if they're opposite sexes, maybe they'll fall head over heels for one another and join the families. Then we'd really be sisters."

"Ah, Claire-bear, you're still just as silly-"

"I thought I'd find the two of you here." My mother strode into the room, her usual regal bearing and clipped tones softened when her eyes met Claire's. With a hand on my old friend's shoulder, she continued. "Your mom's been looking all over for you, honey. I think they're ready to leave. Though I don't know why when it's still so early."

With a wink at me, Claire patted Mother's hand. "Tommy's supposed to get in later tonight. We didn't know for sure until right before we left, so Mom wants to get a few things done at the house before he arrives. You know how it is." She stood, stretched, and then reached out to me. I took her hand and squeezed it, letting go before the inevitable sigh of exasperation from my mother.

"Bye, Claire-bear. Maybe we can get together for lunch before you head back to KC."

"That's a promise." She grinned. "Thanks for coming to find me, Mrs. Randolph." With a jaunty wave she was gone.

I closed my eyes and prepared for the onslaught. Perhaps Mother's concern with being overheard would outweigh her desire to berate me.

"Well, Jessica? Are you getting up and coming to help promote your father or do you intend to hide out here the rest of the evening?"

When I opened my eyes this time, it wasn't just a tiny ripple effect; the entire room quaked. I blinked, hoping the sensation would fade. It didn't.

"I wasn't feeling well." Putting my hand on the nightstand, I pushed myself up from the bed. I swayed toward my mother, so dizzy she was forced to grab hold of my arm to steady me.

"Have you been drinking?" The accusation was spat out in disgust. Her grey eyes bore into me, but rather than making me feel small and ashamed, I wanted to laugh. After all, how can you take anyone seriously when they have three sets of eyes dancing across a distorted face?

"Not a drop. Meds." Standing up must have set off a chain reaction in my body. My brain was as muddled as the room looked, all squiggly and fuzzy. How could the Vicodin have hit so suddenly?

Ellen Randolph, mayor's wife, society matron wannabe, and erstwhile mother of the plain and ordinary Jessica Keller, wasn't buying it. All three pairs of eyes studied me as both of her mouths formed a wry expression.

"Have you eaten anything today?"

I'd been prepared for accusations, not the genuine concern etched in her voice. She could do that, criticize and condemn one second then suddenly switch to kindness and maternal care. Claire and I tried to figure it out, wondered about schizophrenia or some strange form of manic depression. We'd learned all the psychological buzz words, but none of them explained my mother.

"Jessica, I asked you a question." The voice had an edge to it now. There was the mother I knew and loved.

"Um… I—don't remember. Maybe a piece of toast this morning." Could that be right? I wasn't really sure. The days had been rolling into a jumble for so long now that I wasn't always certain which were which.

Except for three days ago. I didn't think anyone could forget seeing the jet crash into the World Trade Center. People commented that 9/11 would be this generation's Kennedy assassination; you'd always remember exactly where you were and what you were doing when it happened.

As Mother led me from the room, it felt as though a spider was crawling down my leg. Pulling from her grasp, I swatted at the area. Something warm and sticky clung to my fingers. I stared at them, confused. In my med-induced fog, my mind was unable to process what I saw.

"Oh, my Lord, Jessica, you're bleeding!" She pulled me through the connecting door to the bathroom, shutting and locking that door and the one leading into the hallway. After rummaging in the linen closet for dark colored towels and wash cloths, she turned me around and unzipped my dress.

"Bleeding?" I obediently stepped out of the dress.

"How could you not know you'd bled through?" She said, checking the dress to see if I'd ruined it.

As she continued to speak, my brain flashed to another bathroom and Jonathan's assault.

Gall boiled up from my gut, threatening to spill out. I gripped the towel rack to keep from falling, thought better of it, then sank onto my knees before the toilet and threw up.

"Your dress is fine, but you'll need clean underwear, hose, and some pads." No words of concern for my getting ill. Just more of the same. "You stay here and I'll bring what you need. But first I need to check the spread." She stared down at me, shaking her head and causing all three sets of eyes to bounce and jiggle. "Couldn't you be responsible and thoughtful just once?"

"But he-he raped me." The words were out before I could stop them. I wanted to flush my head, my entire body, down the toilet. I was terrified she would turn around and reprove me, accuse *me*. But she didn't turn, just held onto the doorknob and remained perfectly still. For a moment I thought she might say something, the expulsion of air, the audible intake of breath all gave me a strange glimmer of hope.

"Clean yourself up. I'll be right back."

So that was that. My confession, a plea for help that slipped out accidentally, had been ignored. If it were possible, I was more alone now than I had been before.

Chapter 3

I sat in the breakfast nook in my parents' kitchen just outside the hustle and bustle of the caterers and servers rushing in and out of the room with trays of hors d'oeuvres and drinks. Once she'd given orders to Manny Ortiz to feed me, Mother returned to her hostess duties. Manny and his wife Consuelo owned the best restaurant and only catering service in town and had been handling these soirees for years. I'd spent a lot of time with them, hiding out in the kitchen and out of the way of the horde of people who always showed up. I wasn't crazy about crowds and didn't want the risk of making a fool of myself just to be reprimanded about it later.

Now, with Consuelo seeing to the needs of the revelers, I was left in Manny's care, and he was determined to have me eat the sandwich he'd set in front of me. I tried to smile and appear grateful for the food, but the thought of it turned my stomach. The variety of smells in the kitchen—from the meats, to the various open bottles of liquor—added to my nausea. It didn't help that the world still rippled and swayed. The initial pain had lessened, and had I been able to sleep after taking the medicine, I'm sure everything would've been fine. Instead, the additional medication left me woozy and sorry I hadn't followed dosing instructions.

"Come on, Jessie, eat up so you can get your strength back." He patted me on the back. "You can't let this get you down. There will be other babies."

It seemed everyone knew about the miscarriage. True, since Daddy was the mayor, anything that happened to members of the family would be fodder for the gossips. Besides, Bennington isn't large enough for someone to get lost. Still, it would have been nice to have a little privacy.

But then Jonathan wouldn't have all the condolences and attention. Both of which seemed to bolster his already enormous ego.

"So, what's going on with our chicky?" Consuelo came over to the table, kissed me on the forehead, then pulled up a chair next to me. "I saw Jonathan a moment ago and wondered if you were here." The slight downturn of her mouth spoke volumes.

"I'm sorry."

"Now, why should you apologize for that man's behavior? If he wants to persist with this nonsense about my name ending in an "o" instead of an "a," let him. If that's what it takes to give him a laugh," she shrugged her shoulders. "Not important. What is, however, is how you're doing." She placed a hand on my forehead then against my cheek. "You're pale but no fever. You don't look like you've been sleeping."

"I've been watching the news on the terrorist attacks. Have you heard about the group on Flight 93 that went down in Pennsylvania?" Tears filled my eyes. "They *k-knew* what was happen-"

"And all involved are heroes, Jessie, the firemen, police, volunteers, everyone—except the black-hearted devils responsible. The heroes and their families deserve your thoughts and prayers, sweetie, but you can't sacrifice your health." She pushed the sandwich plate closer to me.

"I'm nauseous, Connie." Looking into her rich brown eyes, I couldn't go on. Instead, I picked off a piece of the bread and nibbled on it. In the meantime, Manny retrieved a lemon-lime soda from an ice chest and poured me a glass.

"That will help your stomach," he said, setting it in front of me.

"She'd do better with cola, Manny. More soothing for a bellyache."

Manny turned to fetch one, but I called him back.

"This is fine. Really. I promise to try more of the sandwich."

"At least some of the chicken, honey. That'll be good for you." Consuelo added.

"Just let me do it in my own time. Okay?" I smiled at them, loving the care and concern on their faces. "You don't have to babysit me, you know. I'm a big girl now."

"True, but you'll always be my little chicky." She patted my knee. "And you don't like these parties now any more than you ever did." She shook her head as she stood. "I should do another walk-through to make certain everyone has what they need. Manny, you want to give me a hand?"

When they'd gone, I put down the bread and bowed my head; it had suddenly become too heavy for me to hold up. Though taking the extra Vicodin seemed like a good idea at the time, I now realized how stupid it had been. Maybe my mother was right. Maybe I was irresponsible.

"Consu—oh, Jessica, I'm sorry. I was looking for-"

"Consuelo," I nodded, gazing up into the warm, friendly face of my former pastor. "She'll be back in a couple minutes. She and Manny went to check on the platters."

Pastor Nickerson smiled and folded his hands in front of him. "I imagine these fundraisers keep them hopping. Your parents, too. It's been a while since I've attended, so I'd forgotten how—boisterous they can be."

I couldn't help laughing at his expression—and word choice. "They are loud, overpopulated, and quite certainly boisterous. Especially when guests drink too much. Perhaps with you in attendance that won't be a problem."

Now it was his turn to laugh. "Since most of them only know me in passing, I don't think my being here has affected that aspect at all. It appears that overindulgence is part of getting supporters to dig further into their pockets. It might be effective in the realm of politics, but I don't believe it would be as successful from the pulpit. While our Lord partook of the fruit of the vine, He warned against excesses in all things. Even when it might further His cause."

He asked if he could join me at the table, and I agreed with enthusiasm. I'd always liked Peter

Nickerson and hated when Jonathan pulled us out of Faith Community and into a new church. That had been three years ago, and I still missed the close-knit congregation of the church where I'd grown up. After all this time, I still felt like an outsider at Our Mission. And, to be completely honest, there wasn't anyone or anything there I would miss if I stopped attending tomorrow.

"So, how are you doing, Jessie? I don't need to tell you how much we've missed your smile at Faith."

"You just did," I grinned. "And thank you. I miss everyone, too." Which was an understatement. Since joining Our Mission, Jonathan's tendencies toward controlling had steadily headed upward, reaching an all-time high. I didn't blame the church, of course; it was simply an observation.

He'd taken Ephesians to the extreme, demanding submission and subjection as his right as a husband. He'd forced me to quit my secretarial job, limited my contact with anyone outside his circle of approved friends, and taken a "rule of thumb" attitude with me. He'd always been harsh and unforgiving in a lot of ways, but the recent escalation frightened me.

It's too bad he hadn't read a little further, beyond the submission of the woman and into what was expected of a husband toward his wife.

"Jess?"

The steadying hand on mine caused an involuntary flinch. I smiled at the pastor, hoping to cover the reaction.

"Pain meds on an empty stomach," was my offered explanation. "Not pretty, let me tell you. Things are more than a little out of kilter."

He was about to say something when my mother swept in. Her image was still distorted, but not as bad as before, which was a good sign.

Pastor Nickerson stood as she held out a hand in such an affected manner that I wanted to laugh—something I'd never think of doing any other time.

Peter Nickerson smiled and shook Mother's hand, thanking her for the invitation to this event. I could tell from her expression she'd had nothing to do with inviting him. The slight raise of her artfully sculpted brows spoke volumes to anyone familiar with Ellen Randolph.

That left the question of who had issued the invitation. Not Jonathan; he considered Nickerson too old fashioned and uptight. Could Daddy have invited him then? Considering he'd never forgiven the Pastor for not sharing Zach's troubled meetings with him—*before* my brother's death—that seemed doubtful.

"We're so happy you could come, Peter," Mother said in her effusive way. "I hope you're finding the company both stimulating and enjoyable."

"Very much so. It's always good to see the community together like this. You've put together a splendid fundraiser, Ellen. We could use you back at the church."

Mother's lips, though still wrapped around a smile, tightened. She'd never enjoyed attending church. I think she looked at Zach's death and Daddy's anger at Nickerson and God as a way to avoid it completely. Maybe that's why she appeared to be the one family member who'd actually been able to put that part of our lives behind her. She no longer had to pretend to believe in something other than herself.

"Yes, well, perhaps I could give some of your, er, church ladies a few pointers."

"We'd be delighted."

I idly wondered if the pastor wasn't getting some small satisfaction from putting my mother in such an awkward position. All that fake graciousness nauseated me, but that could just be the meds and the nibbles I'd had from the sandwich.

They both breathed a sigh of relief when Consuelo returned to the kitchen. Mother remained next to me while Pastor Nickerson went to talk with Connie.

"Are you ready to return to your duties as co-hostess?"

She'd never considered me as "co" anything… unless that was cohort to my brother's adventures. Zach never personally involved me; I'd been too young. But I'd usually know what he was up to or where he'd gone. That hadn't helped the already tenuous relationship between Mother and me. Still, it gave me some awesome memories of a brother I dearly loved and who had died far too young.

"I'll have the food and drinks waiting in the Fellowship Hall after the vigil tomorrow night, Pastor," Consuelo was saying. "We've gotten so many donations, that my heart is bursting with thanksgiving."

Nickerson nodded. "There's been an outpouring of love and patriotism across the nation. The community churches are banding together and setting up interdenominational prayer chains to pray for victims and survivors. The events of 9/11 won't soon be forgotten."

"You've put together another candlelight vigil?" I asked, pushing back the food and preparing to stand.

"Did you go out at seven this evening and light a candle? I'd wanted to be part of that, but it didn't happen."

"What do you mean? Part of what?" Mother stood aside so I could get up from the table.

"There have been emails going around about having a national vigil since the attacks." Consuelo placed the party tray she was holding on the counter and began to refill it with the little pigs-in-a-blanket she'd pulled out of the warming oven. "It's been on the news and everything. I'm surprised you didn't hear about it, Mrs. Ellen."

The bewildered look on my mother's face was transitory. She was never one to admit not being in the know. Even when she could care less about the situation.

Now, a light seemed to turn on for her. "So that's what you and Manny were up to earlier." She nodded, then the mask she usually wore fell firmly into place. "It's a lovely gesture, I'm sure."

"They say the message went all around the world," Pastor Nickerson said. "On the way over here, I heard there was such an enormous response that those tiny pinpoints of light could be seen in satellite photos. Now, we won't have that ability with our vigil tomorrow night, but I think it will help ease all our hearts a little. I'm looking forward to the fellowship of the entire community. I hope to see you and Gerald there."

"This is such short notice, I," the mask slipped momentarily, the recovery this time quicker than the last. "We'll attend if at all possible."

Unlikely. She hadn't stepped inside a church since

Zach's funeral. She'd even made certain it wouldn't be a problem when I got married. Though Peter Nickerson officiated, we'd held the ceremony in Woodside Park, at least a mile from all the churches in Bennington.

"I'll be there." I was surprised at the firmness in my voice. Equally surprised that I'd made a commitment without first running it by Jonathan. I might be woozy and out of sorts, but I liked the spontaneity and independence being displayed. Maybe I'd retained more spunk than I gave myself credit for.

Maybe there was still some hope...

Mother ushered me out of the kitchen before she could be backed further into a corner by the good pastor. Taking hold of my elbow, she steered me toward the dining room—the last place I'd seen Jonathan.

Though the party hadn't lessened in its revelries, there were fewer people inside the house than a while ago. The only ones remaining in the dining room were Jonathan and the young redhead he'd joined on our arrival. They were seated at the table, his arm wrapped around her chair, their heads nearly touching, obviously deep in discussion.

"Who *is* that?" Though I kept my voice low, it wasn't quiet enough to keep from being noticed.

It was the woman, not Jonathan, who pulled back. Her fair skin instantly flushed, and her hands had an imperceptible tremor as she quickly tucked them beneath the table. Jonathan didn't even change his position. His initial glare altered, however, when my mother stepped further into the room.

"Are you feeling better, Jess?" He made a conscious effort to be civil. I imagined it had a lot to do with the big green eyes and hot little body of the redhead.

"A little." I turned toward the woman, who gave me the impression she'd rather disappear than have to confront the wife. "Hi, I don't believe we've met. I'm Jessica Keller." I held out my hand and was surprised when she took it.

"Vickie Lassan. I just started working at the extension office for Allentown College. We're bringing classes here to Bennington two nights a week. It's part of an Outreach program."

I could tell she was uneasy. It wasn't just the way her small mouth quirked at the corners, or how her eyes darted nervously, but the way she kept talking. Mother's patience grew thin around the time Vickie started to list the classes that were available.

"I'm sorry, dear, but my husband wants to have a word with the family before he gives his address. Would you mind awfully if we stole away?" Mother didn't wait for an answer from the still blubbering redhead. Her expression forbid discussion, and even Jonathan, who believed women were secondary creatures meant to be ruled and kept in submission, knew better than to cross her.

I followed Mother from the room, managed to keep my balance in check, and realized I was only seeing one of everything. Concentrating on my mother's regal form, the elegant neck, the twist of her platinum-colored hair, which was piled high on her head, I didn't notice Jonathan had stolen up beside me.

Or maybe I hadn't wanted to notice.

"Looks like we're headed back to his office," Jonathan's voice was less than a whisper as he grabbed hold of my elbow and slowed my pace. "Any idea what this command performance is about?"

I shrugged my shoulders a little more forcefully than was necessary, jerking my arm from his grasp. From my peripheral vision, I took note of his surprised expression and felt some measure of enjoyment from it. I'd grown increasingly docile and pliant to his demands, had allowed myself to accept everything he doled out. Obedience had been drummed into my core, with the need to please rather than seek any measure of kindness and consideration for myself. All that had been pushed aside and buried beneath a mountain of hurt, frustration, and guilt. It was rare for me to show any of my own personality. Indeed, I often wondered if there was any of it left, if I'd become a shell of the person I'd once been.

All of this, the confession to my mother, pulling away from Jonathan's domineering possession of my arm… was it the Vicodin that unleashed my inhibitions, the alter-ego clambering to be released, or were these last two weeks the final straw?

Daddy was waiting for us in his den, the soft lighting reflected on the warm, oak-paneled walls a welcome sight after the harsh lights throughout the rest of the house. He stopped in the middle of a round of pacing, signaled for Jonathan to close the door behind us, and motioned for us to take a seat. I was the only one who took him up on it.

"Well, Gerald, we're all here while your guests are wondering where you've gotten to." My mother inclined her head in such a way that the diamond studs in her ears caught the light, sending tiny rainbows of color across her platinum-colored hair.

"Most of them are drunk or so engrossed with one another they've forgotten where they are or what they're doing. Allowing alcohol to flow so freely is simply irresponsible, Ellen, especially with your condition." Mother bristled at that, but Daddy pushed onward in spite of it. "Should anyone be in an accident on the way ho-"

"We've started serving coffee, dear," Mother said tightly. "You know as well as I do that people expect to be served their choice of beverages. No alcohol-"

"Would likely bring a better, clearer headed group." Daddy waved away the discussion. He'd never liked confrontation of any kind, so I was surprised to hear him criticize the situation—and my mother. The very fact he brought up her drinking problem was a shock. It was obvious something was on his mind. He pulled out the chair behind his massive antique desk, sat, and folded his hands atop the blotter. After a moment's pause, he gazed up at me.

"I understand you were a bit under the weather earlier, Jessie. How are you feeling now?"

Mother and Jonathan turned to me expectantly. Their desire would be for me to blow off the situation, to assure Daddy I was fine. That's what was expected.

"I'm better now. Still a little shaky, but better." I gave him honesty.

My father nodded, unfolded his hands and absently picked at the corner of the blotter, all the while focused on me.

"Always a trooper, right, Jess? I'm proud of you and should have told you that more often."

When I attempted to interrupt, to protest, he raised a hand to keep me still.

"This family has had its share of ups and downs, and we've done our darnedest to pick our way through them and carry on. But the other day, when you lost our little grandbaby, I realized something I should have recognized a long time ago." His voice caught, bringing tears to my eyes as I saw him struggling with his own emotions. "It's not enough to merely exist, to go through the motions," he spat out the words. "And surviving without truly *living...*"

"Gerald, this isn't the time-"

"It's the perfect time!" Gerald Randolph, the reluctant mayor of Bennington, my daddy, stared across the desk at my mother, his eyes defiant. After a moment, he looked at Jonathan, a determination in his eyes I hadn't seen in a very long time.

"You may not have known him, but you've been around this family long enough to know a little about its forbidden topic of discussion—my son Zach. Silence hasn't taken away the pain, hasn't lessened the loss, or helped any of us forget. Silence is deadly." His attention came back to me. "And what was good enough for your mother and me isn't good enough for my little girl. I'm not going to allow you to go back inside yourself because of this recent loss. You can't continue to build on all the hurt that remains because of Zach's death."

"We have a house full of people." My mother's voice sent a shard of glass through me. She was angry, and that anger would only be aimed at my father temporarily. I would be the eventual target.

"Sir, I guarantee that Jessie and I are handling the situation-"

Daddy rose from behind the desk and shot them

both a silencing glance. Jonathan slunk against the far wall, crossed his arms, and fumed. Mother stood her ground.

"Then get it over with." She said. "You're expected out back in two minutes. I will not be embarrassed by being late." She turned and started for the door.

"I've set up an appointment for Jessie with the new psychologist." The collective intake of breath proved I wasn't the only one startled by the announcement. "I've interviewed the man, and believe he's trustworthy and capable of helping you get past all this."

He silenced the protests with a wave of his hand. "I know none of you are used to my being assertive. I've let a lot of things pass, but not this—not this time." Daddy strode over to me and placed a hand on either side of my chair. "I love you, Jessica, and you're going to get through this and come out on the other side more than just a survivor. You're going to thrive!"

Chapter 4

I was surprised when Jonathan's anger over my father's "intrusion" into our lives failed to initiate one of his rages. He never touched me, hardly spoke to me the remainder of the night. I'd heard him and Mother plotting ways to thwart my father's plan, but I ignored them. The little appointment card gave me a measure of comfort I didn't quite understand, and as I tucked it away in my purse, I knew I'd go see the doctor whether they wanted me to or not.

I hadn't seen Daddy like this in years. He'd become a shadow of his former self after Zach's death. There had been anger toward God and anyone who sought to give him comfort. The anger sustained him for a long time and had been far more acceptable than what followed.

He'd seemed to shrink both in stature and personality. His silence and a sort of disinterest in anything family related wasn't like the father I'd grown up with. Though he remained actively involved at the middle school where he taught history, the rest of his time was spent in his duties as mayor. Always seeking to improve our community, new projects occupied him. From providing solutions to the few homeless in the area, setting up a food bank unassociated with the churches, and rebuilding homes and lives after fires left families lost and devastated, he worked long after others would call it a day. While he gave himself to these people, he'd become a ghost who walked in and out of my life, always on cue, and always without the love and emotional support he'd once offered.

Now, as I watched the pancakes rise for Jonathan's breakfast, I fingered the card in my jeans' pocket and marveled at the change I'd seen in my dad.

After flipping the pancakes, I turned on the burner under a small skillet, sprayed it with the light mixture of oil and flour I'd concocted, and waited for it to warm enough for the eggs. I never ate breakfast, didn't enjoy making it, but it was among the must-do's on Jonathan's lists. He expected everything to be ready and on his plate when he came down in the morning, every day like clockwork, precisely at 6:30. Nothing could be rewarmed in the microwave; that was cheating. Everything had to be fresh, hot, and seasoned to his taste. When he sat down, the morning paper was to be within arms' reach, with me at the other end of the table—whether I cared to eat or not. I'd managed to carry out his decree to the letter these last few years, only missing the regimen the morning I… miscarried.

I cracked the eggs, poured out the contents into the medium heated skillet, flipped out the pancakes onto a plate, folded over the foil to keep them warm, and poured more batter onto the griddle. After checking the time and making sure the eggs were doing all right, I set to work halving oranges and pressing out the juice. When Jonathan made his appearance, everything was in its proper place—including me.

Jonathan took a bite of the pancakes then looked up at me in surprise. "These taste strange. *What did you do?*"

"You s-said you wanted me to use some imagination instead of sticking with the same old same old. I saw the rice flour in the health market the other day and thought you might enjoy the change."

Using his words back at him would have been more satisfactory, but he seemed in a better mood this morning than he'd been in a while. So, telling him that I'd used the initiative he swore I lacked would have been asking for trouble.

"They're—interesting." He took another bite but only after adding more syrup. "Can you use the flour for other things?"

"Sure, all kinds of things. I found the recipe on the library's computer. Would you-"

"Don't use it to make hotcakes again. And you know how I feel about you being on the Internet. There's a reason I keep my office locked." Thus dismissed, I remained silent until he finished eating—everything except the rest of the pancakes.

The remainder of the day was spent in the mundane, ordinary things Saturdays were for. With Jonathan watching me even more than usual, we got groceries, carefully avoided the health market section of the store, ran various errands, then returned to the house. While Jonathan cursed the lack of programming because of continued reports on 9/11, ranting about how this affected *him*, I took the time to straighten my dresser drawers. Though I'd mentioned wanting to attend the candlelight vigil Peter Nickerson had spoken about, Jonathan managed to avoid the subject whenever I brought it up—which made me even more determined to join the vigil.

I started dinner a little before five and was browning hamburger when the doorbell rang. Domino gazed up at me from the corner she was in the habit of occupying while I cooked. She knew as well as I did that it was useless to expect Jonathan to answer the door. That's what he had me for.

My mother swept past me into the house without a word, only a sidelong look of exasperation in reaction to Domino's low growl. She slipped out of her jacket and held it for me to take as she continued into the living room.

I shushed Domino, who lowered her little head and backed away. By the time I located the special, satin-coated hanger Mother supplied years ago, and carefully hung up the faux fur—though an excellent imitation—she was already in the living room.

"Have you thought further about Gerald's outrageous suggestion?" She tapped a gold toned cigarette case against her leg. She knew better than attempt to light up. It didn't, however, keep her from expressing her nervous energy by toying with it.

I could tell Jonathan was perturbed with her abrupt and unannounced presence in our house, but he'd never have the nerve to tell her. She seemed to be the one person in the world he actually respected more than himself. It was either that or be run over by the steamroller she was.

"It's obvious he feels strongly about it." He released the lever on the recliner, sitting it upright. "I've never seen him like that. At least where family members are concerned. He can be rather formidable when he wants, of course, but it's usually in regard to one of his pet projects."

Mother nodded. "He's been acting strangely since Jessica lost that baby. I couldn't get two words out of him yesterday. Every time I called his office to consult about the fundraiser, he blew me off!" She flounced about the room, finally lighting on the edge of an overstuffed chair. She perched her smallish bottom on the arm, shook her head, and huffed out a huge breath. "Nobody blows me off. *Nobody*." Her pointed stare was directed at me. Since it had been a long time since I'd even attempted to stand up to her, I'd no idea what the glare was about.

"I suppose he has more on his mind than usual. This is the first election where he has legitimate opposition. Franks has been talking about bringing in new businesses, especially that carpet manufacturer who's entertained the idea of building here off and on for several years. He has a background in politics, worked on the governor's campaign." Jonathan's admiration for the man was obvious. "Like I said, he's real competition."

"Not for Daddy." I piped in. "You're forgetting the town came to him, begging him to take the job."

"A lot has changed since then. The City Council isn't comprised of the same mentality. These people see expansion as progress and are determined to compete with the surrounding area to bring in new blood. Your dad was the best this town had to offer back then."

"And he's the best now as well!" Ellen Randolph knew how to put an end to a conversation she didn't want to have. The only real evidence of her concern was in the way she continued flicking the cigarette case open and closed.

"We need to get back to the discussion at hand." She said firmly. "I don't believe Jessica needs a therapist. You two can work out whatever difficulties you have, accept the miscarriage, and move on. She doesn't need to air family matters to some stranger."

"I totally agree. I've never had much use for the psychological community. Every time you turn around they've come up with a new disorder and drug to treat it. Besides," Jonathan spared me a half glance. "Jessica's fine. The doctors said so."

I knew what that look meant. I also knew precisely why he didn't want me talking to anyone. I hadn't taken any Vicodin today, but the sense of freedom I'd felt for those precious few hours last night—however loopy they'd made me—had carried into today. I may not be able to say it outright, but I could certainly think it.

I met his eyes with as close to defiance as I could come without fear of what might follow, concentrating on what I'd say if only I could.

Then stop abusing me.

The words jumped from my mind into the air between us but were unable to penetrate his skull. Instead, they continued discussing me and my father's audacity of making the appointment without the courtesy of consulting either of them.

"I'm going." I cleared my throat. "Did you hear me? I'm going."

They stopped speaking and regarded me as one might a child.

"You've no idea what you're talking about, Jessica. This isn't just about you. We cannot have people talking-"

"You think after all that's happened with the terrorist attacks that my going to a psychologist is going to be on anyone's radar?" For a good part of my life I'd tried to convince Mother of my significance, and here I was minimizing it.

"I don't want anything to tinge the public's opinion of this family. Your going into therapy will cause people to question your father's strength."

"I'm sorry to disagree, Mother, but I don't see how." My quiet voice carried across the room and assaulted her. I gulped in a deep breath and wondered what made me actually speak the words.

"Have you heard anything we've said, or have you become so wrapped up in yourself that you don't care how such a thing might be construed?" Mother stood and smoothed the crisp creases in her black linen slacks.

"I-I'm only saying that Daddy must have taken everything into consideration before he approached the doctor. You both know how much he loves this town. He'd do anything for it and has." I tried to relax but wasn't having much luck. "You taught me to respect the two of you, Mother. Wouldn't refusing to keep the appointment be a form of disrespect?"

A well-manicured hand went to her throat, and I could see the pulse in her neck quicken. "Perhaps once wouldn't be so bad." She croaked out.

"I forbid it!" Jonathan flew from his chair. The

startled look on my mother's face didn't even faze him. "Gerald had no right to make such a decision on his own. You're not his little girl; you're my wife, and I will not have you blabbing personal information to some shrink. It's no one's business but ours, *and you will not keep that appointment.*"

He'd come across the room to where I sat on the sofa, his entire visage reflecting the thunder of his words. He didn't make the effort to skirt the coffee table; he knew he didn't need to. His message was loud and clear.

Domino shivered at my feet, steeling herself for the upcoming attack. Though she knew better than to come between Jonathan and me—he'd kicked her out of the way more than once—she always kept watch, waiting, I thought, for a chance to attack him.

I reached down and petted my little dog and, out of the corner of my eye, saw my mother approach. The slight look of alarm was still visible in the quirk of her mouth.

"Technically," she said, placing a hand on Jonathan's shoulder. "A shrink is a psychiatrist. The gentleman in question isn't a medical doctor but a Ph.D. He can't prescribe drugs but is supposed to be trained as a therapist."

She wasn't saying anything Jonathan didn't already know, but I recognized what she was doing. I'd seen her sidestep things to diffuse situations in the past— between Zach and my dad.

Jonathan appeared to relax. He drew away from the coffee table and strode into the connecting dining room. Once there, he turned back to us.

"I don't see the use of this. As far as I'm

concerned, there's no reason to continue the conversation."

Mother was about to answer him when I realized I'd left the hamburger simmering. Before hearing her remark, I scooted out of the room, Domino close on my heels. It didn't matter. I'd already made up my mind.

All the incentive I needed was in what Daddy said the night before. He wanted this for me, to help me. It might not matter to the others how I felt about the loss of my baby, but it mattered to him. That was enough.

After draining the hamburger and checking to make certain it hadn't scorched, I combined catsup, mustard, and a handful of other ingredients to make the sloppy joes. I was just putting the finishing touches to a salad of baby greens when the phone rang. By the time I picked up the receiver, Jonathan had already answered the call. Turning back to the stove, I was startled by my mother's appearance in the doorway.

"It looks like you're getting your way." Her mouth turned down in disgust. "That was your father. We'll be attending this candlelight vigil as a family."

Chapter 5

We met in the sanctuary of Faith Community Church a little after seven. There were people waiting with baskets filled with candles and directions on what was about to happen. Throughout Bennington similar scenes were underway, choreographed down to the smallest detail. From St. Mary's Catholic Church on the south edge of town, to Danner's Gas Stop on the north, with designated points east and west, a circle of candles would be lit and held for fifteen minutes before everyone would make their way to Veteran's Park in the middle of downtown.

We dispersed immediately, following the directions to our specified location. Daddy and Mother held hands as they walked in front of Jonathan and me. I could hear them whispering, their voices so quiet I couldn't make out what they said. I doubted she had warmed to the idea of participating in the vigil, but she appeared to be making the best of the situation.

As for Jonathan, he'd been giving me the silent treatment since my mother's announcement regarding our attendance at tonight's event. Though he didn't usually carry on much conversation during our casual Saturday night meals in front of the TV, he always had a comment on something. Tonight, however, there had been nothing—not even an occasional accusatory glance in my direction.

He'd been civil to my parents and everyone we encountered, giving the impression it had been his intention to be part of the event all along. Only I knew the truth and had to wonder the price I'd pay when it was over.

It was a wondrous thing, watching as the candlelight grew from one candle to the next, each person sharing his flame with his neighbor. I heard whispered prayers, quiet sobs, and the shuffling of feet from those who were uncomfortable—like Jonathan and my mother. There were no loud voices, just a sense of respect and reverence.

Later, as we made our way to the park, I saw my father rush ahead of the crowd, Mother following closely behind. I'd no idea what was going on and, at that moment, didn't care. I shielded my candle from the breeze caused by the movement of so many people, kept my mind focused on our collective purpose, and stayed in step with those around me.

The tiny pinpoints of light from hundreds of candles lit up the night where only a sliver of a moon shone. Sure, the streetlights helped, but I let my imagination carry me along, believing that our candles and prayers were shoving aside the darkness and fear the terrorists had hoped to inflict.

A stage equipped with a microphone had been set up in the middle of the park. My parents and several members of the local clergy were assembled there, waiting patiently for the crowd to fall in around it.

Father Clarence Hardy came forward and, after testing the mic, thanked everyone for the show of support. He said a brief prayer, then introduced my father. Daddy came to the front of the stage with a somber expression. Gazing out over the crowd, the corners of his mouth raised slightly, his eyes narrowed in a look I recognized as one of extreme concentration. He raised his hands to settle the crowd.

"As Father Clarence stated, we are overwhelmed by this truly spectacular show of support." His voice rang out strong and clear. "Bennington has done herself proud tonight, and I want each of you to remember that *this* is what America is made of. We are a nation formed under God, blessed by God, and dedicated by our faith and belief in Him. People who attack our citizens, our country, and threaten our way of life cannot win. As long as we remain strong and focused on what we as a country stand for, they cannot succeed. They may threaten us, they may overwhelm us by their cruelty, shock us by their show of force, and try to demoralize us... *but we will not be shaken in our resolve*. This is our land, these are our rights, and until God gives up on us, *we will not fail*. We'll mourn our dead, support our survivors, heal as a nation, and demand a reckoning from those who seek to destroy us. For we *are* "one nation, under God," that is our strength—*that is our right*."

There was no applause, that would have been impossible while continuing to hold the candles, but the crowd did show its appreciation and agreement to what my father said.

It started out quietly but gradually picked up power, growing louder and louder until the whole valley seemed to quake from the intensity, bouncing off the not-too-distant mountains and returning with even more strength and purity of purpose. It didn't matter who started it; the message was clear.

God Bless America.

~~~

Jonathan and I returned to Faith Community and joined my parents in the Fellowship Hall where refreshments were provided. Various other churches throughout town were likewise set up, which made it even more surprising that Our Mission hadn't joined in the community effort. I didn't question it, happy to be back in my old stomping grounds.

Even though my father hadn't been inside a church in eight years, he seemed comfortable—far more than I expected. Mother, however, was considerably ill at ease. Though she retained that plastered-on smile she donned whenever campaigning with Daddy, it was obviously more forced than usual. And every time one of the "church ladies" spoke to her, I imagined her response was through gritted teeth.

Jonathan remained at my side, for once not grasping or pinching my elbow. Perhaps it was the press of all the people, or maybe the scene at the park had affected him the way it had me and so many others. It was another of those little things to be thankful for.

"Hey, Cookie!"
~~~

I searched the crowd, finally spotting Claire and her husband. Jonathan was so engrossed in a conversation with someone, I managed to slip away without him noticing. I'd worry about repercussions later.

We gave each other a hug then weaved our way through the crowd and up to the sanctuary. There were only a few people here, which was a welcome sight after the elbow to elbow crowd. We selected a couple of pews, Claire and Tommy taking one in front of me.

"Wasn't that incredible?" Claire's rich brown eyes glowed with excitement. "I'm so glad we were here and able to be a part of it all!"

"You don't think they did this in Kansas City?"

"I'm sure there were several vigils throughout the city," Tommy responded. "But it was nice to be in our hometown, you know?"

I nodded, afraid if I spoke I would reveal just how much their being here—not just for the vigil, but here in Bennington—meant to me. If only for a few stolen moments, I was able to bask in the glow of my friends' smiles and the company of Zach's best friend.

I studied Thomas Lofgren, Tommy to all, and remembered the times he and my brother teased and tormented Claire and me. Though most of it had been done in fun, there'd been a kind of rivalry between them that I hadn't understood. Claire, always ladylike, even when we climbed trees and broke into their fort in the woods, had been adept at flirting long before we were really interested in boys. She'd even determined that one day she would have to choose between them for a husband.

Had Zach's death forced her to choose the

remaining friend?

Glancing from one to the other, I knew that had not been the case. These two really loved one another. It was obvious with every look, every touch. I wondered what that was like, how it felt to have someone care so much about you and feel the same for them. I felt a twinge of jealousy creeping over me and shoved it aside. I'd made my bed as the saying went…

"So, how long are you guys planning to stick around?"

"I've got to be back in the office Monday," Tommy said. "But Claire's staying on a few days. You girls need to catch up and make arrangements for you to come visit us, Jess."

I'd heard those words many times since they'd moved away. Whenever I'd asked Jonathan if I could take them up on the invitation, he'd nixed the idea. If he didn't go, or want to, then there was no reason for me to do so. It wasn't something easily explained to people who didn't live the way I did.

Claire and I were firming plans to get together Monday morning when Jonathan found us. His greeting was warm enough on the surface, but I recognized the furrows across his forehead. He wasn't a happy camper.

Rather than risk his further displeasure, I cut our conversation short, gave Claire and Tommy hugs, and followed Jonathan out to the car. He didn't speak, and I knew better than to try and draw him out.

I sent a silent plea heavenward, begging for mercy.

And at least one night without abuse.

Chapter 6

Jonathan's cold shoulder attitude continued through church the following morning. He spoke with me only when absolutely necessary—which wasn't all that unusual. His concentration was focused on those who were considered the high muckety-mucks of the community—which included Vern Franks, the man running against my father. I'd no idea what he saw in Franks, but I rarely understood what motivated Jonathan. I figured it all came down to who could help him the most in his current pursuit of interest. That left the doors wide open in my estimation. Remain on my father's side as long as he was the one in power, but make certain the opposition saw how valuable you could be should things go their way. Or maybe he was just being a spy in the enemy's camp. I didn't know and knew he'd never tell me.

While he made nice with the natives, I stood by quietly—and obediently—just like the other wives who knew their place in the scheme of things. Several of the women came over to ask how I was feeling, offered their sympathies, then moved further away from the men and began their own conversations about children, church-planned events, and the like, all in the usual subdued tones that showed they gave deference to the males. Though it always bothered me to some extent, today it shot home how vastly different things were at Our Mission when compared to Faith Community. And I didn't think it was just my skewed perspective.

When the men finally had enough of their posturing, Jonathan took hold of my elbow and steered me from the building. The moment we were in the parking lot, he dropped his hand, wiped it against his pant leg, and proceeded ahead of me to the car.

I glanced at the sleeve of my blouse, wondering if I'd gotten something on it, but there was nothing there. It was obvious he was still perturbed about the therapist appointment and Mother's insistence that "once, just to satisfy Gerald" wasn't a request he wished to honor. He may have a grudging respect for my mother, but it didn't mean he liked following her lead. Ordinarily, he'd have made his feelings crystal clear, standing his ground if he strongly disagreed. For some reason, he could get away with that when dealing with her. Perhaps it was because the incidents were rare. This time, however, his acceptance of her decision bothered me. I didn't understand his reaction and had to wonder when the pout would change to violence. The thought sent icy tentacles up my spine.

While I made his lunch, Jonathan changed from his church attire then positioned himself in front of the TV. His anger over the cancellation of sporting events was instantaneous—and unsettling. I didn't dare say anything, though I'd have liked to. Instead, I held my tongue and remained in the subservient role that was expected.

After placing the tray with his lunch on the side table next to his recliner, I waited nearby to see if he'd want anything else. Though we had a standing routine on Sundays, him watching a game of some sort while I took a few hours off to visit my grandmother, today was far from ordinary. His anger and insensitivity over what he perceived as a personal affront to him—no games, no standard programming—could change everything.

But standing up to Granny Ed would not sit well with her. Jonathan despised my grandmother but knew better than to cross her.

I'd no idea what transpired between them; their animosity toward one another was obvious, which made his consent to this arrangement odd. His acquiescence may have been tempered by the fact that she was my maternal grandmother but more likely because he believed she had money.

"Do you need anything else?" I asked him now, anxious to leave.

Jonathan glanced over the top of his water glass and rolled his eyes. He took his time, watching me as he paused between swallows.

"Have you got dinner planned?"

"Already in the Crock-Pot. Stew," I said, anticipating the next question.

Yes, he let me go to my grandmother's but not easily. He seemed to find a particular enjoyment in delaying my visits. He'd found out just how far he could stretch it before Granny Ed fought back. He hadn't enjoyed the cops coming to the door to check on my welfare.

Of course, I hadn't enjoyed the aftermath of those occasions, either.

"You've got three hours—and that includes driving time." He finally answered. "Don't let the old bat try to convince you to stay, Jessica, or…" He allowed his voice to trail off, flashed a grin that filled me with dread, then turned back to his food.

I gathered up Domino, grabbed her carrier, and was in the garage in a heartbeat. On a good day, it took a minimum of fifteen minutes to get to Granny Ed's seniors' community. I prayed for a good day and light traffic.

Granny Ed's condo was the first one as you entered the complex. In spite of rules that limited individuality, Edna Collins had made the outside of her home just as unique as she was. Next to her front porch sat the tiny grotto she'd formed from native stones which contained a fresco of Christ's birth. The artwork was her creation, done during a fast right before Zach's death. She claimed it was why one of the angels looked remarkably like my brother: God had given her forewarning of what was to come.

I pulled up her driveway, waved to her neighbor Nellie Roth, Nosy Nellie as Granny called her, grabbed Domino, and got to the door without being forced into a big discussion.

I felt Nellie's sad eyes follow me the entire way. When she came across her almost nonexistent front lawn, I knew what was coming.

"Are you doin' okay, honey?" Nellie called out as I

rang the doorbell.

"I'm fine, Mrs. Roth, thanks for asking." I smiled at the woman, hoping she'd keep her distance. I knew her eyes weren't very good, the thick glasses alone revealed that, but I also knew what this former school counselor was capable of. She had a heart of gold and a sixth sense that could denote a problem—or a potential one—a mile away.

"You always did minimize your problems, Jessie Randolph." It wasn't an accusation; the sympathy in her expression told me she could see deep into my soul. That was not a place I wanted anyone privy to—least of all Granny Ed's neighbor.

The door swung open behind me, and my eighty-year-old whirlwind of a grandmother swept out onto the little porch.

"Why, Nellie, is that you lurking over there behind my granddaughter's car?"

"I don't lurk, Edna Collins." Nellie pulled herself up and stared defiantly at her neighbor.

I controlled the impulse to laugh at these former best friends. Up until the Valentine's Day dinner earlier this year, the two had been inseparable. Then, a "gentleman" who'd recently moved to the complex had shown interest in both women. From that moment on, they'd been in competition over an eighty-four-year-old Romeo who was likely having the time of his life stringing them along. Of course, Granny Ed summed it up in her own inimitable way, "It isn't every day that you find a man his age with all his faculties, teeth and hair included!" There wasn't much you could say to that.

"Come on in here, Jessie," Granny Ed took hold of

my arm, flashed Nellie another cold, hard glare, and tugged me inside. "I imagine that husband of yours has the timer counting down, so I don't want to waste our time on that old busy-body."

Once inside, I gave my grandmother a hug, then released Domino from her carrier. The little mixed breed terrier nearly jumped into my grandmother's arms when she bent down to say her hellos.

"There's a sweet girl," Granny Ed stroked Domino's head and allowed herself to be the recipient of several sloppy kisses. "Wish this silly place'd let me have a pet. But no, huh-uh, can't do that. I've even taken them proof of how caring for a pet can keep seniors healthy." She shook her head, her snowy curls dancing a jig. "Can't make them see sense 'cause they think they know everything."

"Not everyone keeps such an impeccable home," I told her, looking out across her sparkling living room. "You're an anomaly, I'm sure."

Her harrumph was answered by a yip from Domino. We both followed her into the small kitchen where Granny Ed set down bowls of food and water for my little dog.

"Looks like you've been shopping," I said, indicating the packages stacked neatly on the table and a couple of chairs. "Which of your charities?"

"No charity this time, sweetie pie. You." She raised her eyes to mine and held them. "You know how I am, can't sleep 'cause of that darned insomnia. Anyway, I was watching TV and came across a story about how these people were caught in a snowstorm. That's when I started thinking about you."

I stared at her confused. "I've never gotten-"

"True," she nodded. "But there's always the possibility, Jessie-girl. We live in a mountain valley, and who knows what could happen. At any rate," she lifted the largest package and set it in my arms. "Now you'll be prepared. You still wear a ten, right?"

"Yes…" I eyed her suspiciously. "Granny Ed, you know how Jonathan hates when you give me gifts-"

"When it's not your birthday or Christmas." She finished for me. "I've no idea what your mother sees in him. He's an idiot." She waved her hand toward the package I held. "Besides, these aren't gifts, they're… necessities."

Necessities, like the cash she'd surreptitiously slipped in my purse over the years, a secret between the two of us. Not only was Jonathan not to know, but neither was anyone else. Especially my mother. Though it made me uneasy, the thought of refusing her gifts and hurting her was worse. Still, when I'd been forced to quit my job, I'd asked Granny Ed to keep the money for herself. She hadn't questioned me about the request, never said a word, which was more than a little surprising.

She'd always been generous to Zach and me while we were growing up, giving us special gifts or what she referred to as a little "spending money." Zach said it was her way of making up for how strict she'd been with Mother; that by spoiling us, she felt it made amends for the past.

"Don't just stand there staring at me, Jessie Lynn, let's get busy!"

I ripped open the paper wrapping and did a double take when I saw what was inside: a bright yellow coat smashed inside a sealed plastic bag.

"I-uh, thank you, but I don't do yellow."

Granny Ed nodded as she took the item from me, slit the plastic, then shook out the vivid yellow concoction. Like magic, it doubled in size.

"It's a down parka." She said with a kind of pride as she handed it back to me. "Let's see how it fits."

I unzipped the coat, and dutifully followed her instructions, hoping it didn't show how much I disliked her gift.

"It's a little big," I commented, zipping the parka.

"It's a fourteen, I think." Granny checked the fit, turning me about so she could examine it.

"Seems a bit bigger than that."

"Just as well. It'll do nicely."

"Granny Ed," how could I say this and not hurt her feelings?

"Um, sweetie?" She helped me out of the parka and placed it across one of the kitchen chairs. She grabbed up another package, then turned back to me expectantly.

"I'm not overly fond of yellow. Especially such a bright yellow." I breathed out, mentally crossing my fingers that it didn't hurt her feelings.

"It *is* dreadful, isn't it?" She patted the hood of the coat before handing me the next package.

"You don't like it either?"

"Oh, heavens no, Jessie! But it'll serve its purpose, and that's what counts. Come on, open that one." She clapped her hands together like a child at Christmas.

I didn't stop to question her odd statement, figuring she'd get around to telling me what was going on. I ripped open the package and discovered a pair of cotton long johns—extra heavy and one size larger than I'd normally wear. Not that I'd ever worn long johns or thought about doing so.

The "gifts" kept coming and the items stacked up to make an impressive collection of cold weather gear. Fur-lined snow boots, insulated gloves and socks, two wool sweaters—neither my size, one larger than the other, as well as a very large pair of flannel-lined jeans and a belt. I tried everything on under Granny Ed's watchful eyes and nodding approval. When the last item had been placed with the others on the table, my grandmother presented me with her old picnic hamper, an over-sized basket with flip-top lids on both sides and duel handles. Inside, I discovered what looked like a couple of stadium blankets and one of the old coffee tins she collected.

I cocked my head and looked at her expectantly.

"Those are special insulating blankets. Lightweight but guaranteed to keep out the cold. As for the tin, it's for the candle."

"The candle?"

"Um." She answered, digging in her slacks' pocket.

"So, that's it, then." I stared at the stacks of clothing, still more than a little confused.

"Well, almost." She handed me a list along with a check. "I want you to promise you'll get these things and put them in your trunk so everything's together." She patted the picnic basket. "Most will fit in here."

I scanned the paper, then gazed up at her. "I know how you like everyone to think you're quirky and eccentric, but we both know that's not the whole story. You're the sanest person I know."

"Why thank you, Jessie Lynn." She winked at me

and continued folding and stuffing things into the hamper. When she got to the parka, she released a heavy sigh and sank into the chair with the coat on her lap.

"I imagine you want an explanation."

"That would be nice." I pulled up an empty chair and sat down. Domino hopped onto my lap after discerning my grandmother's was too full. "Are you expecting me to camp out in the wilderness or something?"

She shrugged her thin shoulders. "Not expecting anything, sweetie. Just making sure you're prepared for anything that comes your way." She fingered the soft material of the coat for a moment before continuing. "That program I told you about, well, it didn't have a happy ending. But it could have.

"You know, most people just go about their business in the winter with the willy-nilly notion that nothing's going to happen to them. But when you live around mountains as we do, it's a good idea to be prepared for the unexpected."

"I always carry a shovel, sandbags, and a really thick rope. There's also a quilt and a heavy-duty flashlight."

"Gerald's idea, I'd wager." She nodded and grinned at me. "Those can be handy, I'm sure."

"And all this?"

"You keep in your trunk along with the other things." She held up the bright yellow parka. "This wasn't so you'd look pretty, Jessie, but so you'd be seen. Kind of like hunters wear those orange vests. They're not attractive, but you're not likely to be mistaken for an animal."

"Maybe a giant yellow canary," I laughed.

"Yes, well, not in these parts." She reached across the table and took my hands in hers. "I want you safe, sweetie. And yes, I know you're not usually off by yourself, but if you are, then you'll be prepared. And," she went on before I was able to say anything, "You don't have to worry about asking Jonathan's permission for any of it."

I didn't argue with her. It wouldn't have done any good.

"Now," she said, peering intently at me. "I want you to tell me how you're *really* feeling. None of that lip service Ellen and Jonathan insist on."

Considering she spent very little time with either of them, it was surprising how well she knew them. As for me, lying to Granny Ed was never on the agenda. Even half-truths didn't ring true to her. Though, for the most part, she'd let those slide. Thank God she never pressed for more information about my marriage and relationship with Jonathan. That was one truth that could be dangerous for both of us.

"I'm getting better each day," I said finally. "I, well, to be honest, I'm almost relieved I lost the baby. I'm sure it's for the best."

She stared at me long and hard before saying anything. "God knows what's best, Jessie; we've got to trust that. Though you and I both know that sometimes things are taken out of His hands because a person's choice may not match the Almighty's."

I knew she was referring to Zach. It wasn't something I was prepared to talk about. I'd worked hard to avoid the subject since it happened eight years ago.

"It just wasn't the right time," I told her, hoping to

veer the subject away from possible discussion of my brother. "We weren't ready to be parents."

I knew she realized there were things I wasn't telling her, but, thankfully, she didn't pry.

It had taken a long time to get through her survival gear, and I needed to get back home. She helped me load everything into the trunk of my car, extracted my promise that I'd get the things on the list, then sent me on my way. As I headed toward Jonathan and home, a wonderful warmth spread throughout my body. Granny Ed's gifts might be a little out of the ordinary, but every one of them spoke of love.

Exactly what I needed.

Chapter 7

Jonathan was so considerate when I got home that I felt the urge to check the house number to make certain I was in the right place. It had been years since he'd done *anything* in the kitchen, but while I was gone, he'd put together one of the boxed bread mixes we had in the cabinet and set the table for supper. I couldn't help eying him in suspicion when he placed candlesticks on the table and found the tapers that went into them. After he lit the candles, he urged me to wash up so we could eat.

A little thrill of hope and excitement ran through me. Was this the answer to all my prayers? Had Jonathan finally realized the error of his ways, how horribly he'd been treating me?

"Please, Father. Please." I prayed as I washed my hands and ran a brush through my matted curls.

The assault the night of the party had been the worst abuse I'd suffered at his hands—with one exception... He'd been harsh and cruel in the past, yes, but never had he inflicted everything at once as he did that night. Perhaps it had been the breaking point, the thing that turned him around and changed our lives for the better. Perhaps…

Jonathan had everything on the table when I returned. He'd set it with the china we'd received as a wedding present—something we'd used perhaps twice in our four years of marriage. He'd lit the candles, and with the ambient light coming from the kitchen and living room lamps, it reminded me of the early days when Jonathan had worked hard to impress and romance me. In spite of everything that had come between that time and now, I found myself responding to the setting, my confidence to answered prayer high.

"It's lovely," I told him. The breathless quality of my voice brought a smile to his lips. He held out a chair for me, gallantly seating me first before settling in at the head of the table.

"The wonderful smell of the stew inspired me." He took my bowl and filled it. "Is that enough or would you like more?"

"It's great, thank you." I touched the linen napkin in wonder, closed my eyes for a brief prayer of thanks, then spread the napkin across my lap.

Before serving himself, Jonathan cut a slice of nut bread from the still steaming loaf, placed it on a plate, and handed it to me. I thanked him, barely able to breathe, wondering at this dramatic change in him. Even when we were first married, he'd rarely served me, or thought of me before himself—especially when it came to meals. Yet, deep inside, there was a niggling feeling this was all a ruse, that he was playing me. I wanted so much to believe in the transformation that I pushed those thoughts aside.

The moment he took his first bite of the stew, I thought everything would be undone. His face screwed up, his light blue eyes were hard when they looked up at me, and I went cold. I tasted the stew and knew immediately what was wrong: in my haste to get to Granny Ed's, I'd been too careless with the seasonings—predominantly the salt.

"I—I'm sorry, Jonathan. I can fix you-"

As I reached for his bowl, he took hold of my hand, surprising me by the gentleness of his touch.

"Sit, Jessie. It's fine." He forced a smile that gradually seemed to soften. "The bread will tone it down. See?" He took a bite of the bread to prove his word.

I settled back into my chair and followed his example. After a few more bites, the ice water with lemon seemed to cut the saltiness of the stew. I relaxed, determined to enjoy this "new" man in my life.

I couldn't remember the last time we'd actually engaged in any kind of congenial chatter, but that's what happened now. As Jonathan told me about a program he'd watched on a weather channel, I listened avidly. His enthusiasm caught me up, and I found myself smiling. Really smiling.

"So," he said, "how was your visit with Edna?"

There was an imperceptible edge to his tone, but his face didn't show any signs of it.

"In rare form, as always. She'd seen some kind of program telling of the dangers of winter driving."

"So her solution was…"

He'd eventually see all the stuff in the trunk of my

car. If I told him now, while he was in such a good mood, there was a chance I'd avoid his anger.

I put my spoon down and looked over at him. "She went on a spending spree and bought me a survival kit."

There it was, the tightness at the corners of his mouth, the narrowing of the eyes. I braced myself for what was certainly about to come.

"Really? She doesn't think Gerald's insistence that you carry a shovel and sandbags is enough? You did remind her that I just bought you a new car."

I gazed down at my plate, wishing I hadn't been so foolish and ruined this nice dinner—and brought about the return of the man always filled with so much anger and hate.

"It—it's a little more complicated. All about keeping warm and, um…" I glanced up at him, surprised to find him still seated and not looming over me. "You know how she can be, how eccentric she is. I mean, for goodness sake, she bought me a bright yellow parka she knows I'll never wear, just to keep in the trunk of my car!"

"Yellow? On you?" I tried not to flinch when he reached over and picked up a strand of my auburn-colored hair. "That's gotta look good." He dropped the curl and laughed. It was so light-hearted, so engaging, I couldn't help but laugh as well.

"I've got to admit I wasn't brave enough to even look! Oh, Jonathan, wait till you see the stuff. It's all over-sized and, well, functional, but nothing I'd ever actually wear or even want. But it seemed so important to her for me to have the things." I felt badly talking like this about my grandmother's gifts but knew if I acted like it was nothing, like it was just more of her eccentricities, as Jonathan insisted on calling her actions, then he'd be more apt to allow me to keep everything.

"Knowing Edna, she'll check every week to make sure you've still got the junk in the car." He shook his head and made a visible attempt to regain his former convivial attitude. "To keep her from going completely around the bend, you may keep the items. But I really wish you'd try to discourage her, Jessica. As a matter of fact, I don't know why your mother hasn't taken the issue up with a lawyer. Edna's faculties are shaky at best, and these spending sprees and fears of hers are getting out of hand."

I knew better than to disagree with him, even though it would be obvious to anyone who examined Granny Ed that she was more cognizant than most people half her age. And as far as my mother trying to control Granny Ed—she'd have to be in a coma and unable to defend herself for that to happen.

"Yes, Jonathan," I lowered my eyes, obedient and respectful. "I'm sure Mother's tried."

The atmosphere was charged, ripe for one of his rants, but a sudden smile and a sparkle in his blue eyes diffused it. One of his hands snaked across the table to caress my arm.

"I don't blame you, Jess. Relax." He reached out to gently stroke my cheek. "Eat your dinner, sweetheart. After the dishes are done, you can dig out one of those old movies you like so much and we'll watch it together. How does that sound?"

It sounded like an answer to prayer. Still, I couldn't help wondering what was going on and questioning this remarkable change in attitude.

Just go with it, Jessie. I told myself firmly. Go with it and enjoy while it lasts.

After all, with Jonathan, everything was transitory.

Chapter 8

I checked out the large candles, searching for something thick and tall that would take a long time to burn through. Smell was a big factor since I was sensitive to strong odors. If, God forbid, I was trapped inside the car, I certainly didn't want anything with a heady scent.

"What are you looking for?" Claire picked up one of the candles and sniffed it. "Oooh, I like this one. Just a hint of vanilla." She placed it beneath my nose. "What do you think?"

"After a few minutes, the smell would be so strong, I'd have to put it out." I shook my head. "Don't they make anything these days without a scent?"

"That's what most people want." Claire's rich brown eyes crinkled at the corners. "You're just so blasted picky!" She giggled.

It was good to be out with her, to talk and tease one another. It had been a long time since I'd felt so relaxed in anyone's company. There was nothing to prove with Claire, no worries about how I'd be perceived. It was easy to slip back into our old relationship, where trust was understood, and secrets were what we told one another, not what we kept from each other. I prayed that things I withheld from her would not interfere with what we had, that our time together wouldn't be tainted by the intervening years and Jonathan Keller's penchant for abuse.

"Do you see anything that says "emergency candle"?" I continued to check the labels on the larger candles.

"Um…what about this?" Claire held one up that looked far too small to be of any use. "It says it's supposed to burn thirty hours."

"Huh? That little thing?" I took the proffered candle and, sure enough, the label touted its longevity.

"How many do you want?" Claire grabbed another one off the shelf.

"She has down here three, but I doubt she knew they made anything like this." I checked my list, ticking off one more item.

"Never underestimate Granny Ed." Claire pulled another candle off the shelf. "If she says three, we get three." She set them in the shopping cart then peered over my shoulder at the list.

"All purpose-"

"Lighter." She held up the item. "Cross it off as well. And don't forget that first aid kit we picked up in the pharmacy. It's a nice one, too," she grinned. "Granny Ed would be so proud. Now, give me a gander at that list again." She peered over my shoulder. "Um… light sticks and flashlights would be over near automotive, tissues, toilet paper, bottled water, granola bars, and probably the matches would all be in grocery. We should pass by the pantyhose on our way. As for the pocketknife and rope, um, maybe camping. You have any idea what light sticks are?"

"I'm not sure, but someone here has to know. Maybe all those things would be in the camping section." The face I made got her giggling.

"Wherever! Thank God for Bennington's Every Little Thing Marketplace and one-stop shopping!" She placed a hand on her swollen abdomen and grimaced. "Gotta be a boy," she said. "Every time I shop he kicks in protest."

We both laughed. I shoved the grocery cart, the crazy wheel on the front screeching in protest. Claire disappeared down an aisle in housewares and came back with a pack of special heat-resistant hot pads.

"Don't want you to catch the interior of your car on fire, now do we?" She tossed them into the cart. "You've gotta remember to show me that parka. I didn't know All Weather Gear had anything like that."

"Down?"

She shook her head. "No, silly. That color of yellow!"

As we passed by electronics, Claire let out a squeal and I grabbed onto her, worried she'd gone into labor. She shrugged off my concern and pointed to what had gotten her so excited. I followed the line of her finger and gulped in astonishment.

"He *said* they were recording, that they'd be in the stores soon. I never realized how thrilling it would be to actually see it like this!"

She rushed over to an enormous display for a

hometown boy who'd made it to the big time. Eric Whitney's haunting green eyes stared out from the poster, reminding me of a time I tried hard to forget.

While I attempted to catch my breath, Claire examined the back of the Whitney's Connection CD. She kept bobbing up and down, bringing to mind the cheerleader she'd been. Though I couldn't bring myself to pick up a CD, neither could I keep my eyes off Eric's paper ones.

"I just love *Saving Grace*." Claire cooed. "You've heard it, haven't you? *"You are my one love, my Saving Grace"*," she sang with a smile.

The following lines were imprinted on my memory from the only time I'd heard it on the local station. *"But loving you meant leaving her, so very hard to choose."*

From what I remembered about Eric, and I remembered *everything* about my former boyfriend, the choice hadn't been that difficult for him.

And contrary to his lyrics, his decision had nothing to do with me or God.

"I've heard it once." I told her, finally able to find my tongue.

Claire set the CD in the cart, seemed to think about it for a moment, then picked up another one.

"Tommy and I went to see them at a church in KC. They were playing a benefit for a family whose daughter was dying from cancer. The little girl had seen them before, and when asked the one thing she'd like to do, a special wish, she said she wanted to go to another Whitney's Connection concert and meet the band. When Eric heard about it, he broke down and cried."

"You told me." I hadn't meant it to sound so cold and hoped my words were softened by the touch on her arm and my smile. "I'm glad he got his dream. I know how much it meant to him."

Claire gazed at me a moment, then gave me a hug. "I'm sorry, sweetie. I know it hurt when he left."

I patted her shoulder. "Ancient history. Right now, we have a survival kit to put together."

A final look at the poster of the only man I'd ever really loved—an admission that was still hard to make—and we were back on course.

We picked up the remaining items on Granny Ed's list and loaded them into the trunk of my car. I'd have to box them up later, but for now, I put the stuff out of my mind, determined to enjoy the time with Claire.

We'd met at McDonald's earlier that morning. She'd had a craving for their hotcakes. And since I wanted more time with her, it worked out perfectly. After the incredible evening with Jonathan and congenial breakfast that morning, I was flying high, no longer waiting for the other shoe to drop. And getting to spend time with Claire—with Jonathan's permission— was icing on the cake.

Before I was allowed to close the trunk, Claire removed the bright yellow jacket and examined it.

"Well, I've gotta give Granny Ed her props, Jess. It does look like it'll be warm. And she's right, you'll stand out—even in the woods." She crinkled her small nose and shoved the parka into my arms. "Glad I'm a flatlander now. No need for all this gear."

I tossed the coat into the trunk and shut it before she had the chance to dig into any more of my grandmother's survival kit. "Better be careful, or I'll tell Granny Ed how cold it gets in Kansas City and how much you have to travel to get from one place to the next. I've got your address, and-"

"Don't even joke about a thing like that!" She ducked inside the car. "Seriously, though," she said when I was settled behind the steering wheel. "I'd like to see Granny Ed before I have to leave. What do you think about going over this afternoon?"

"Can't today, but you're welcome to pop in. She'd love to see you." I wondered what she would think about my father's unusual gift. My initial reaction was not to tell her—that's the way Jonathan had conditioned me. But when I looked over at this dear friend and remembered all the secrets we'd shared throughout the years, a dam inside me broke. "Daddy's arranged for me to speak to a therapist. Isn't that a kick?"

Claire's eyes grew large. "*He* arranged it? Ellen didn't stop him?"

I shook my head and started the car. "She didn't know anything about it until he dropped the bombshell the other night—at the fundraiser, no less. She and Jonathan were about to jump out of their skins at the suggestion." Oops, I'd said a little too much. Maybe she wouldn't notice.

"Jonathan doesn't like the psychiatric community either?"

She'd noticed my faux pas. "He just doesn't think there's a reason for me to see anyone. That's all."

I couldn't tell if she bought my explanation. From the corner of my eye, I saw her settling back against the seat, but that was about it.

"What about you, Jess? Do you think you need to talk to someone about losing the baby… or anything else?"

I wouldn't allow her words to sting, refused to get

into a deep discussion that would eventually turn to Zach. Instead, I ignored the last words of her sentence and shrugged my shoulders. "I don't know. It was really hard at first, but I'm coming to terms. There's no other choice, after all. But the fact Daddy thought enough about me to make the appointment says a lot."

"So, you're going."

"Yep, in spite of my mother's protests, I'm going."

Chapter 9

There was a sign on the door that said to come in and take a seat. The minute I opened the door to Dr. Matt Harris's office and heard the voices, I nearly walked back out. I stood half in, half out of the outer office, looking toward the open doorway to the inner sanctum.

"So, you see, doctor, it's imperative that I know immediately if Jessica's become unstable. After what happened with her brother..." Jonathan let the sentence hang, the implication making me want to shout denials. But I remained transfixed, unwilling to reveal my presence.

"I assure you, Mr. Keller, if your wife seems at risk, I'll refer her to the proper med-"

"That's all well and good, but in the meantime, Jessica could hurt herself. No, no, I *insist* on being kept in the loop here. Look, Dr. Harris, Matt," the switch from harshness to camaraderie meant Harris wasn't giving in to Jonathan's bullying. It might be possible to like this man after all.

"You have to understand where I'm coming from. Jess has become sullen and secretive since the miscarriage. I've tried talking to her but haven't been able to get through."

"Then it's a good thing she's coming to see me. I understand your concern, but you've got to respect the confidentiality of my position-"

Not wishing to be caught eavesdropping, I closed the door quietly behind me, scooted down the hallway, and slipped into an elevator that was about to close. I'd no sooner settled against the rear wall when the door slid back open.

"Jessica." Jonathan's startled voice and expression went on my all-time list of best times ever.

"What are you doing here?" I asked, careful to keep it from sounding like an accusation. Since we'd been getting along so much better, I didn't want to risk spoiling things.

"I came to show my support." He took my arm and led me from the elevator. "When you weren't in reception, I thought I'd go to the first floor and see if I could catch you."

When had he gotten so good at lying, or had he always been this way? I gazed up at him, smiled, and held my tongue.

"Are you nervous, Jessie? Because if you're having second thoughts…" He had his hand on the doorknob, waiting for my answer.

"No, I'm fine." Keep your resolve, I told myself, taking a step forward. I don't know what I expected but was a little surprised when Jonathan opened the door and let me pass. He stepped in behind me, took my elbow, and *gently* turned me around.

"You're being a good daughter to follow through. I get that now. After everything your parents went through because of your brother, I know you don't want to let them down."

I swallowed hard and felt the gorge rise in my throat. This wasn't a topic of conversation I wanted to pursue. He knew this, knew how much it hurt me. But his voice was tender, *tender*, not harsh and cold like it usually was. And the touch on my elbow, the careful way he'd turned me to him... Wasn't this proof of love?

"Ah, Mrs. Keller, how nice to meet you." The owner of the voice I'd heard earlier now came toward me with a hand outstretched in welcome. I went forward to meet him and shook his hand.

"Dr. Harris." He had a warm, firm grip and his dark blue eyes were kind and sincere. I liked the way they crinkled at the corners, like he was always smiling. He had dark hair with a small amount of gray sprinkled throughout. I wasn't good at guessing ages but figured him to be in his late thirties, early forties.

"Hi, I'm Jonathan Keller, Jessie's husband."

I couldn't believe he continued the farce, going forward and shaking Harris's hand like they hadn't just been talking. For the doctor's part, he registered surprised, which placed another plus mark in his corner. Harris was obviously uncomfortable with Jonathan's playacting, especially with the look Jonathan gave him of raised eyebrows and the slight incline of his head toward me. Even I could read the meaning of that.

"Well, sweetheart, I'll leave you in Dr. Harris's

capable hands." Completely out of character, Jonathan kissed me on the mouth, touched my cheek, then turned to go. "It was nice to meet you, doc. Take care of my girl, now."

I followed Harris into the inner office and gazed about me a bit surprised. It looked more like someone's living room than an office.

"Find a seat that's comfortable, and we'll start getting to know one another. How does that sound?"

"Like you intend on seeing me more than once." I hadn't meant for it to sound so nasty, but it was an accurate assessment. I turned back to the living room grouping and chose an overstuffed chair. It was opposite a large sofa and had a coffee table filled with magazines between them. And would be a nice, safe distance from wherever the doctor sat.

"Your dad's prepaid for ten sessions, Jessica—do you mind if I call you that?"

"Ten?" It was mind-blowing. If only Daddy had followed through when seeing a therapist would have done the most good. But Mother had thwarted his efforts to get Zach the help he needed.

"He wants to make certain you're all right. We all do."

I figured he was referring to the meeting he and Jonathan had earlier. They must have come to some kind of terms, like him sharing whatever I talked about. Wasn't that against the rules, a breach of ethics?

Harris took a seat on the sofa opposite me. He had a file folder and legal pad in his hands. He pulled out a sheet of paper from the folder and handed it to me along with a pen.

"I'd like you to fill this out if you could. It's just a

few questions that will help me in evaluating your needs."

"You want me to do it now? Because I really don't intend to be back."

"Fair enough." He nodded, his expression thoughtful. "But I don't want you to make a hasty decision. This time is yours for the next ten weeks, all paid. I'll tell you what; you take the paper home and if you should decide to return next Monday, just fill it out and bring it with you. That sound all right to you?"

I took the paper from him, folded it, and placed it in my purse. I sat with my legs crossed, my hands in my lap, looking at nothing.

"So, what would you like to talk about?" Harris eased back against the sofa. He no longer held anything, just sat there gazing at me.

"This is crazy," I shook my head. "I know Daddy is worried about me, and I think that's awesome, but this really isn't necessary."

"You know how fathers can be. They see their child suffering and want to fix it. Sometimes it just takes longer for them to realize they can't do it alone."

There's no way this guy could know anything about what my family had been through. Sure, Jonathan had been talking to him about Zach, but even Jonathan didn't have the whole story.

"You said I could talk about anything, right?"

"Yes, I did."

"Okay... How did you meet my dad?"

Harris twisted on the sofa and his expression suddenly appeared guarded.

"We actually met at Wilton's Coffee Shoppe."

He didn't flinch, so that was the truth.

"So, you two just started talking?"

"In essence, yes."

The man smiled in a way that made me feel he knew a lot more than he was willing to say. Still, there was something about the look on his face. The smile was real, friendly. There was nothing imposing or demanding about his expression or his posture. Yet, here I was, bristling all over, wanting to attack.

The idea brought to mind something Claire said a long time ago, about my being able to let loose and get angry at her because it felt safe. It was true of Claire, but how could there be a comparison between her and this man I'd never met?

The sincerity of his gaze was too much. I looked away and scanned the office. It was decorated with an ocean theme in mind. Lighthouse prints and models filled walls and shelves, which held shells of all kinds. On the coffee table between us was a beautiful little shell with spines and whorls of the softest pink. The shell was inviting, giving me the strongest desire to pick it up and examine it more closely, but I resisted the urge. Instead, I stared down at my hands twisting in my lap, wondering how long this farce appointment would last.

"What else would you like to know?" Harris's voice broke in on my reverie, and I looked up to find him still smiling at me.

"I, um, I... How did my father come to the conclusion I needed to see you?" There, it was out, the burning question I'd waited three days to ask.

His eyes never left my face, though his smile appeared to take on a less exuberant appearance.

"He came to me after you lost the baby. Asked my

opinion."

"And you, of course, told him to send me right along."

"Actually, no. I suggested he keep an eye on you, see how you were handling things. I wasn't sure he should be making the arrangements."

"Really? That's surprising, considering you told Jonathan you'd keep him apprised of what we talked about."

My accusation seemed to stun him. But only for a moment.

"Ah, you were here." He nodded. "I'm not sure what you think you heard, Jessica, but I want to assure you that nothing you say will ever leave this room. What you choose to talk about stays here, between the two of us."

"But you said-"

"The only thing I guaranteed your husband was that if I felt you needed more help than I could give, I'd see you got a referral to someone who was better equipped to handle your needs." He leaned forward, hands turned upward, outstretched and open. "I share nothing, Jessie. Not with your father, not with your husband. Not only would that be highly unethical, but it would be wrong morally as well."

Every fiber in my being screamed he was telling the truth, that I should open up to him, spill my guts. But while I believed his words and heart were in the right place, it wasn't easy for me to trust anyone.

I may not know what was going on in my marriage, but there was one thing I was certain of: I'd be seeing this man again.

Chapter 10

The mild September weather was followed by even milder October days. Knowing how quickly the weather could turn, I made the most of it, taking several long walks with Domino each day.

Though Claire and I hadn't spent much time together, when she went home to Kansas City, it left a giant void in my life. The continued sessions with Dr. Harris helped—even though I spent more time interrogating the therapist than actually sharing anything about myself. Still, it was a welcome change from the mundane routine of cooking, cleaning, and laundry which Jonathan had long ago decreed were to be done daily. And with Daddy's popularity dropping in the polls, Mother insisted on dragging me from luncheon to luncheon, campaigning. I'd never understood politics and had no desire to figure out the intricacies involved. I participated because that's what was expected of me.

Not that I wanted Daddy to lose the election; he was the best man for the job. Vern Franks was a slick, fast-talking piece of work who thought his vice presidency at Danner Oil and Gas—comprising countless gas stations throughout the region—gave him a leg up over a middle-school history teacher. I was sure if anyone cared to look more closely at Franks, his reputation as a hard-nosed, rear-kissing, know-it-all would make him low man on the totem pole. As for his position at Danner, it didn't hurt that he'd married the owner's daughter, whereby landing the position, qualified or not.

Jonathan continued to cozy up to Franks every Sunday after church. I was suspicious about the relationship just as I was confused about much of what was going on. The rigid schedule Jonathan always adhered to, like the meticulous accountant he was, no longer appeared to matter—at least when it came to what he did after he left for work every morning. While I was expected to abide by his rules and cook meals he didn't eat, he'd been staying out later and later, not coming home for supper or calling when he was going to be late. He rarely spoke to me, frequently slept in the guest room, and hadn't touched me in weeks. I didn't mind the last part, but it *was* curious. I wondered if it had anything to do with my sessions with Matt Harris. I never broached the subject, however, fearful it might lead to one of his tirades.

As I made Jonathan's breakfast and reflected on my new "normal," I thanked God for the peace of the last few weeks and prayed it would last.

"Where'd you get this?" Glaring, Jonathan tossed something on the counter in front of me.

One glance at the object had my breath catching in my throat. Sunlight bounced off Eric Whitney's CD, a parting gift from Claire.

Stay calm, keep the peace.

"Claire thought I might like it."

Jonathan's harrumph spoke volumes. He knew all about my old boyfriend. With Eric out of the picture, I'd been left at the mercy of my mother and her protégé, Jonathan Keller, both of whom were determined to control my future.

I remained focused on the skillet, refusing to give in to the onslaught of memories. I waited for him to say something else, for him to break his all-time record of congeniality and resume with his habitual abuse, but he simply turned and walked to the table. I served his basted eggs and toast, then sat down opposite him while he ate.

"I understand Whitney's going to be making the rounds here in Bennington."

I'd seen the announcement in the paper the night before about Whitney's Connection joining with several area churches in fundraising efforts for 9/11 survivors and disaster relief.

"I read something about it in the paper." I wrapped my hands about my mug of hot chocolate, waiting for Jonathan to spew his venom and get it over with.

"Is he any good?"

The comment took me by surprise. "Um, I—don't really know."

"Didn't you sing with the group he had in high school?"

"That was a long time ago. But, yes, I did."

Jonathan looked up from his eggs and stared at me.

"So, was he any good?"

"I always thought so. Though I'd no idea he'd make it this far."

He didn't say anything more, just finished his breakfast and left for work.

Domino watched while I loaded the dishwasher, likely hoping something would spill onto the floor so she could grab it. When the phone rang, it startled both of us.

"Jessie, Peter Nickerson here. I wondered if you might have time to come down to the church in a little while. I've a proposition for you."

"Now what might that be, Pastor?" I laughed.

It was an unexpected pleasure to hear from Pastor Nickerson. I'd thought a lot about him and Faith Community since the candlelight ceremony in September. Thanks to my "talks" with Matt Harris, I was gathering the courage to approach Jonathan about returning to my old church. I wasn't quite there yet, but I was working on it.

Though I never discussed personal things like the miscarriage, Jonathan, or anything else too painful to delve into, we had spoken about my faith and what I missed in the church we now attended. Matt was a firm believer that being part of something like a church congregation went a long way in helping people heal. And I fully agreed with him.

"I'd explain over the phone," the pastor continued, "but am afraid it wouldn't be as effective as a face-to-face." I sensed the smile in his voice and knew there would be an ornery twinkle in his eyes.

"I have to admit to being intrigued."

He chuckled. "So, what do you say, Jessie, do you

have time to come down this morning?"

My regular Monday meeting with Matt Harris wasn't until two, so aside from housework, I had nothing planned. Visiting with Peter Nickerson might not be on Jonathan's strict agenda, but there was no way I was going to pass up the invitation. And since Jonathan wasn't keeping track of my odometer as he had in the past, this out-of-the-ordinary trip shouldn't be an issue.

"I can be there in an hour. That okay with you?"

I could hear him conferring with someone before he came back on the line.

"Sounds great. See you then."

In between mopping the kitchen floor and getting cleaned up to see the pastor, I fielded calls from my mother. Unfortunately, her new cell phone acquisition gave her a kind of unlimited access to me that she hadn't possessed in years. She reminded me of a luncheon later in the week then called back a few minutes later, questioning me about today's session with Matt Harris.

"I suppose you're keeping the appointment."

"I am." After nearly a month, I'd thought she'd give it a rest. The derision in her voice proved otherwise. There'd been no rumors circulating as a result of my sessions, but maybe she believed Daddy's fall in the polls was somehow connected to me seeing Dr. Harris.

"I would think you'd be over the miscarriage by now, Jessica. You were barely four months along. It's not like losing-"

"Zach?" I finished for her. "No, not like that." I found my voice catching on the words as a vision of my brother popped into my head. How many times in the last few weeks had I thought about talking to Matt about my brother? How many times had I stopped myself short, afraid the therapist's eyes would grow cold and hostile and he'd point a finger at me and declare I was to blame? Even though I knew that wasn't his style, more my mother's, I'd still been unable to open up about Zach.

Or about Jonathan.

"That was unkind, Jessica."

"I know, Mother," I said, closing my eyes and squeezing back tears. "I'm sorry. I didn't mean-"

"To hurt me? You're doing it more and more lately." Her haughty tone made me wish I hadn't apologized. "Jonathan said you've become increasingly aloof and unapproachable. Can't you see how much you're hurting him?"

This was not a conversation I cared to continue. Since I knew she was on her cell phone, a simple reminder that people might hear the conversation was enough to get her to sign off.

And gave me a moment to collect myself before I headed to the church.

Chapter 11

The first person I saw when I entered the Fellowship Hall was Granny Ed. She had her back to me and was in an animated discussion with someone I couldn't see. Her snowy hair danced about her head as she nodded and laughed with the other person. I figured it had to be Pastor Nickerson, so I thought nothing about it as I continued into the room.

"There's my girl now," Granny Ed turned to me, revealing her companion, a pleasant looking young woman I didn't know. "Jessie, meet Arabella."

"Bella, Mrs. Collins." She held out a slender hand. "It's nice to finally meet you," she smiled.

I took her hand and returned the smile. "Finally? What's my grandmother been telling you?"

"Everything." Granny Ed giggled as she gave me a quick hug. "And if you're Bella, I'm Edna." She shivered. "Though I'd rather you call me anything but that. Always hated the name."

"Hence, Granny Ed," I joined in. "She was very particular about what we were allowed to call her. Aside from that little quirk, she's one incredible lady."

"I could see that the moment we met," Bella grinned. "I've a feeling we're gonna be best friends in no time."

"Ah, go on with the two of you." Granny Ed blushed. "Bella sings with Whitney's Connection, you know."

Don't react; just keep smiling and play the game. And there was a game afoot, that was certain.

"I do right now. Sing, I mean. Don't know how long this morning sickness is gonna let me continue." Bella tossed her long, pale blonde hair and sighed. "I'd no idea it could actually last all day. Ugh." She patted her slender stomach.

The tight feeling in my chest extended throughout my entire body. From the mention of Eric's group, it felt constricted; now it was bone-crushing. My fight or flight instinct urged retreat, but doing so would mean my feet needed to move. And, at that moment, with Pastor Nickerson and Eric Whitney coming toward us, breathing was difficult.

Peter Nickerson's words were blocked by the buzzing in my head. My eyes were fixed on Eric's, his on me. As memories tore through the barrier in my brain, spilling out in a messy concoction of emotions and scenes from the past—the way his dark hair fell over his forehead, the glint in his green eyes... I wondered if he remembered or felt anything at all.

"Jessie?" Pastor Nickerson touched my elbow, bringing me back to the present in a rush.

"I'm sorry, did I miss something? I just

remembered an appointment I have to keep." Granny Ed's sharp senses discerned the lie, but she didn't say anything.

"That's too bad. We were hoping to-" The look that passed between my grandmother and the pastor brought him up short. "I understand if you have to go, but I'd hoped you might help Edna and me set up the donation booth. Don't know how it happened, but we're shorthanded this morning."

He may not know how it happened, but I was fairly certain I knew the answer. A sweet, often meddlesome, eighty-year-old woman determined to have her own way. One look at Eric Whitney told me I was right.

I made a show of studying my watch, wondering how to leave and not hurt the pastor's feelings.

Or stay and risk a confrontation I wasn't prepared for.

"I'll be glad to help a little while." A decision. Maybe not the best, considering the fact I still had the tightness in my chest, but it was the right thing to do.

"We can help, too. Right, Eric? Just tell us what you need." Bella didn't wait for agreement, seemed to expect him to cooperate. And the way she looked at him showed an intimacy between them.

Better not go there.

Bella threw herself into the project with so much enthusiasm it infected the rest of us. The pastor and Eric set up a large table near the entrance to the Fellowship Hall while Granny Ed directed Bella and me to assist in gathering everything from paper and poster board to the special cloths to cover the tables. Once the process began, it was the proverbial well-oiled machine, coming together quickly. We were so deeply enmeshed in setting up the donation booth there wasn't time for anything but the job before us. No time to stew about how I'd been led here today, no time to do more than exchange an occasional glance with Eric. It wasn't until Pastor Nickerson asked if Eric and I would help him arrange the rows of chairs that we finally spoke to one another.

"It's good to see you, Jess," he said quietly while the others hung before and after pictures of the World Trade Center site. Against that stark background, what I felt about him, his betrayal of my trust, was not only petty, but ridiculous.

"It's nice of your band to donate your time like this."

"When I mentioned we'd be in the area, Pastor Nickerson asked if we might carve out some time to help with fundraising efforts. It was a no-brainer."

The attempt at conversation was awkward, almost painful. It wasn't surprising, of course, just fact. I'd no other choice than to accept his decision to leave town without me, thought I'd come to peace about it. I had. In a way. Blocking the memories had been easy until Whitney's Connection was on every radio station. Even then, I'd refused to allow thoughts of the past to invade my mind. There was, after all, the all-encompassing demands of Jonathan Keller.

We were saved from further interaction when a couple of men joined us—one of whom made a beeline for Bella. Recognition and shock had my throat tightening once again.

"You're supposed to be taking it easy!"

"Hi, darlin'," Bella stood on tiptoes to kiss the tall, dark haired man I'd recognized. "And I was takin' it easy, you old worrywart." She grabbed his hand and turned him toward Eric and me. "I want you to meet Jessie."

Bella led Paul Hillyard to where I stood, still clinging to a folding chair. All the emotion I'd been hiding, the shock of how my grandmother used the good pastor to lure me here, the shame, denial, and hate I'd held back these many years, boiled inside me. I don't know how I managed, but I remained standing as the man who'd witnessed my brother's last desperate moments of life drew closer to me.

Calm. Please, dear God, help me remain calm!

I sensed Eric behind me, closer than before, like he waited for me to fall so he could catch me. I wondered why he would do that now when six years earlier he hadn't thought what might happen when he left me behind.

"This is my husband Paul," Bella beamed. "I think he knew your brother."

The activity in the room stopped. I saw Granny Ed making her way toward me, a worried look on her face. I drew in a deep breath and forced a smile.

"It's good to see you again, Paul." I tried to release the chair but couldn't quite manage it.

"It-it's nice to see you, too." His voice was strained, his face a study of confusion. I could imagine him wondering if I would scream at him as I had that fateful day, demanding why he hadn't been able to save Zach. That *had been* his job as an EMT, right?

I'd lived with Jonathan Keller for four years now; if it had taught me anything, it was to keep my emotions in check. Deny, deny, deny.

I smiled, released the chair, and held my hand out

to Paul.

It was the right thing to do. The right time. Even if it gagged me.

But it didn't gag me. Instead, I threw myself into the middle of things, right alongside my former boyfriend, Bella, the man who'd been unable to save my brother, Granny Ed, and Pastor Nickerson. We were all determined to make the charity event as inviting, and provoking, as possible.

When they were ready to set up the stage where the band would perform, I excused myself and made my way out of the church. I slipped past Pastor Nickerson with a smile and a wave but wasn't as fortunate with my grandmother. I knew she wasn't far behind me, and though I really didn't want a confrontation, it was evident she wasn't about to let me leave before speaking with me.

"Don't be angry with Peter, Jessie. he didn't-"

"Know it was a set-up?" I kept my back to her, concentrating on my breathing.

"It had been so long, honey, I thought perhaps it might make you smile."

My snort stopped her in her tracks. Still, I didn't turn around, didn't need to since I could see her reflection in the car window as I unlocked the door.

"It wasn't meant to hurt you. Oh, Jessie, can't you see that it's time for you to snap out of this, this false world you've been living in?" She grabbed hold of the door and reached out to gently stroke my cheek. "I've kept my mouth shut long enough, Jessie Lynn. It's high time you own up to the abuse you've been going through."

My shock must have shown in my face.

"Did you think I didn't know, honey?" Her sweet voice broke. "The others may be blind, but not me." She released the car door and stepped back. "It's time you opened up to that therapist, Jessie-girl. Time to get this out in the open and stop denying what's been happening. You deserve better than this."

Before turning to walk away, her eyes filled with tears. Stunned from her revelation, I just sat there awhile, unable to think, to move.

As I drove toward the hospital annex and my appointment with Matt Harris, it felt as if each of the carefully constructed walls built to protect me had begun to crack. What would happen if they crumbled to nothingness?

My jaws ached from gritting my teeth, my brain from having the dreadful secret I held exposed.

I needed help. But was I strong enough to ask for it?

Chapter 12

Granny Ed *knew*. How could that even be possible?

Duh! Of course, she'd have guessed with all the controversy over my seeing her every Sunday, the time constraints... What else had I given away without realizing it?

Sitting in the parking lot, debating whether or not to keep my appointment, I pounded my hand against the steering wheel until a passerby knocked on my car window to ask if I was all right. Mortified, I reassured the woman I was fine, all the while praying this incident didn't get back to my mother.

It's not that I didn't want to share with Matt Harris, especially now I felt he could be trusted. No, it was years of conditioning that held me back. That, and the embarrassment it would cause my parents... and me. And the humiliation. How could I live with that? How could I let anyone see what I'd become, a scared little animal trapped inside a cage without the key, strength, or power to escape.

I knew deep down inside that I wasn't to blame for Jonathan's behavior, that the fault lay with him and him alone. Or did it? Could my inaction be misconstrued as permission for him to treat me so badly? The shame alone was a good reason to maintain the secret.

But Granny Ed knew. And she wanted me to tell Dr. Harris.

I shoved my way out of the car. She didn't understand the implication of her request. She couldn't understand unless...

Just the thought of my grandmother having been involved in a similar relationship infuriated me. She was so small, so... Determined, strong, resilient. Now, anyway. I knew very little about my grandfather. Granny Ed rarely spoke about him, and when she did, it always seemed to upset her and make her sad. As for Mother, I couldn't recall any mention of her father. Odd, perhaps, but in the context of my mother, normal. My grandmother and I needed to have a long conversation.

But that would have to wait. Right now, I needed to face Matt Harris.

Chapter 13

The waiting room wasn't designed for more than a couple of people at a time. It was small, cozy, with two comfortable chairs and the same ocean/nautical theme as his office. The walls were tastefully decorated with paintings of lighthouses and sailboats. I knew all of this from previous visits. Now, I traversed the small space over and over, looking at nothing, my mind racing.

What would I say? What *could* I actually share with him without fear of repercussions?

Granny Ed's betrayal—for that's exactly what it had been—and Eric's attempt to create a normalcy between us after all these years, topped by the sudden appearance of the man who'd been by my brother's side as he lay dying... It was too much for me to handle. Too much.

The door to the inner office popped open, startling me. Matt Harris held the door more closed than open.

Not a very welcoming sign, especially when I needed one.

"I'm running a bit behind. It will only be a couple more minutes." He studied me, his dark eyes intense. "That won't be a problem, will it?"

I shook my head, not trusting myself to speak. He stood there for a moment longer before withdrawing back into the office, reminding me of how a turtle's head retreated into its shell.

It gave me more time.

For what?

I sank down onto one of the chairs, closing my eyes, willing myself to remain calm, to rebuild the crumbling walls in my mind. By the time Matt Harris called me into his office, some semblance of composure had returned.

"I'm sorry to have kept you waiting. There was-"

"No need to explain." I forced myself to sit in my usual chair even though the urge to pace this larger room was overwhelming.

"You seem different today."

A statement not a question. And one that said he scrutinized every move I made.

"I've no idea what you mean."

An imperceptible raise of his eyebrows told me he doubted my response. "Probably just me." He took a seat on the sofa, started to open my file, then set it on the coffee table between us. "How about we just talk."

"Isn't that what we always do?" I smirked.

"Actually, no. I'm the one who ends up doing all the talking. It's more like you're the therapist, and I'm the client."

"I don't consider myself a client." More like a

captive, I thought. Still, a better term than patient.

"My point is that you probably know more about me than I know about you. No comment?" He leaned forward, hands clasped, face far more serious than I'd seen in the prior three sessions. "Feel free to chime in any time, Jessica."

"Are you always like this after the initial get-to-know-you time is over?"

"Nope. You see, most of my clients, or however you wish to refer to yourself, actually like visiting with me. It helps them feel better about what's bothering them."

"I'm afraid if I ever start talking, I'll never stop." A whisper. No, barely a whisper. Totally involuntary. Perhaps he hadn't heard.

But he had.

"There's no need to be afraid-"

"I didn't mean-" It was no use. "I've never spoken about it to anyone." About what? There was so much to choose from. Which was safest?

"Not even your husband?" He leaned back against the sofa. "How could that be? The loss-"

"The miscarriage? You're referring to... No, I mean, yes, we've spoken. I'm not," I couldn't sit there any longer. I got up and went to the farthest side of the room, away from Harris and his prying eyes.

"Okay. Subject closed. For now." He cleared his throat. "There's something I've been wanting to ask you about. Something I've observed."

Deep breath. Calm. Don't tense up.

I turned toward him. "What's that?"

"You don't have to discuss it, of course. The last thing I want is to upset you."

Sincerity. In his voice, on his face.

"Go on?"

"I've noticed you never call Jonathan your husband."

A true statement. "He prefers it that way." Not necessarily true, but why would I call him my husband when I didn't even think about him that way? An admission that should have surprised me but didn't.

"But he *is* your husband."

"Of course." I shrugged, frowning at the direction the conversation was headed. I slowly made my way back to the chair and sat down. "Don't you think this is rather a ridiculous topic? Jonathan is Jonathan. Just as he likes it."

"Um. What about you? Do you like it that way?"

Though my insides squirmed under his penetrating glance, I tried hard to remain still, hold things in check.

"When Jonathan's happy, I'm happy." I swallowed the acid that rose from my empty stomach. "I'm sorry, but you'll need to excuse me. I need some water."

"No need to leave; I've got a bottle here." He got up and quickly retrieved a bottle of water from a fridge somewhere behind his desk.

"I take it you didn't eat before coming today."

I shook my head—a little difficult when trying to sip the water.

"Busy morning?"

I knew what he was doing, trying to diffuse the situation by changing the subject. I was all for it.

"The usual housework followed by a... treat." That was one way to refer to what happened. I took another sip of water. "My grandmother and Pastor Nickerson asked me to help prepare Faith Community's

Fellowship Hall for a fundraiser to help survivors and first responders of 9/11." I know I winced, hoped he hadn't noticed. I was determined not to give in to the crazy onslaught of emotions trying to force their way out into the open. I *had* to get out of here. I needed to go home, cuddle with Domino, and regain control. *Before* Jonathan got home.

"Aw, yes. The Whitney's Connection concert Wednesday night. Will you be going?"

"Probably not." Change the subject. "We don't attend that church."

"I don't think it really matters, especially since you were kind enough to help get things set up. Or is it because you don't like their music?"

"The music's fine. We, Jonathan and I, well, last-minute isn't our style." If I got up now, would he let me go or try to stop me?

"I see."

What *did* he see? I tried to penetrate beyond the dark blue gaze and into the brain beyond. He would have none of that.

"So, tell me what you're afraid of, Jessica. What it is that would keep you talking once you got started?"

My mouth dropped open. It felt as if the muscles in my jaws had become unhinged.

I fumbled for the water bottle, suddenly forgetting how to open the stupid thing. Next thing I knew, Harris was beside me, lifting the bottle gently from my hands to open it for me. He sat in the chair a few feet away. Not quite as far as the sofa, which I'd have preferred.

"I don't-"

"One thing, Jessie," he urged. "You're safe here."

"Safe? Like Zach should've been?" Anger,

frustration. I glared at him. "It's my fault he's dead."

"How's it your fault?" He didn't skip a beat.

"Because I wasn't there." I slammed the water bottle onto the coffee table.

"Was it your turn to watch him?"

"You're not making any sense, twisting my words." I flew out of the chair. "He said he was going to make sure things were right this time, that I wasn't supposed to worry." I grabbed my purse from the floor and flung it over my arm.

"I'm just trying to understand, Jessie. Please sit down. We need to talk about this."

"This? *This* is the problem." I went the opposite way around the chair than I'd ordinarily have gone, just to be further from him. "You're a nice man, Dr. Harris, but this isn't working for me." I headed for the door.

"Don't go, Jessie. We can work through this. One step at a time." He stood but didn't move toward me. "You've obviously had a bad day, something happened to bring all this to the surface."

I turned away, determined to get out of there. Jonathan and Mother had been right; these therapy sessions weren't necessary. They just made everything worse.

Matt Harris met me at the door, a business card and flyers in his hand.

"It's okay, Jessie. I understand. Here," he held the items out to me. "No obligation. Just take a look at the information and remember I'm still here for you."

"Yeah, thanks." I took the things before walking out the door.

The further I got from Harris's office, the stronger and more in control I became. By the time I got to my

car, the internal walls of protection started to mend.
It would be okay. I'd be okay.
I had to be.

Chapter 14

When I got home, there wasn't any time to sit and unwind while cuddling Domino. A quick hug as she went in and out of the back door was all I could afford.

There were three messages from Mother, one from Granny Ed, and one that scared me to death: Jonathan. While he frequently called during the day to make certain I stayed on task with my chores, I'd never missed one of his calls. That, and the kind of day I'd had, terrified me.

Mother's calls were easy since every message was the same: a commitment to attend some sort of luncheon as a show of solidarity for Daddy's re-election. We'd already had this discussion, and I wasn't in the mood to have it again. Still, I returned her call, confirming I'd be there Thursday as promised.

"Eleven sharp, Jessica. Not a second later."

I told her I'd meet her in the lobby of the restaurant at 10:45, which was met with a curt "You'd better," and the click of her phone when she hung up.

Granny Ed asked if I'd call her later in the evening, which might or might not be possible. A lot would depend on Jonathan's mood. Which meant I couldn't ignore his message any longer.

"I don't know where in hell you are, but you'd better be home when I get there."

I'd no idea what I could've done to elicit such a message and wasn't anxious to find out. The only thing I could do was make sure he had his favorite dinner on the table when he got home and pray this wouldn't be the start of another cycle of wrath.

Grilled pork chops, baked potatoes with plenty of sour cream and chives, frozen, French-cut green beans, slowly cooked with liberal chunks of bacon, and smooth, sweet applesauce, waited for Jonathan's arrival. The moment I heard the garage door open, I got everything out of the warming oven and began placing them in their proper positions on the table.

Jonathan stormed into the house, his face a color of red I'd never seen before. But I recognized the fury in his ice-blue eyes. He tossed his briefcase onto the chair next to the door so forcefully it skittered across the surface and landed on the floor.

That would be my fault, too.

"You're to inform your crazy grandmother never to call me at the bank again. Do you hear me?" He growled, rushing forward. He didn't even wait until I'd set the dish of green beans on the table to take hold of my arms and shake me. Both the dish and beans flew from my hands.

"I'm sorry. I'll make certain it doesn't happen ag-" His face was inches from mine, the icy stare freezing my soul.

"The stupid witch wouldn't hang up until I agreed to allow you to attend that concert with her Wednesday night." His grip tightened. "Do you have any idea how embarrassing that was? Hanging up on her didn't work."

"I don't know what to say. I'm sorry." Why would she do that?

Because she doesn't really know.

Jonathan pushed me backwards so hard, I landed on the floor. With a single sweep of his arm, all the food on the table flew to join me.

"Get this mess cleaned up, Jessica. I'm going out."

Before heading for the stairs, he went over to where Domino shivered in her corner of the kitchen and shoved her into the middle of the mess.

"And keep that stupid dog out of the kitchen!"

Once he was upstairs, I rushed to Domino to console her. I knew he'd clean up and change his clothes, but had no idea how long it might take him. The best thing for my dog was to be out of sight by the time he returned. Though I'd have to give her a bath later, right now I needed to get as much of the applesauce and bits of potato out of her long fur as I could before shutting her in the broom closet until after he'd gone. This took a bit longer than I'd hoped, and I'd only just gotten her into the closet when I heard him on the stairs. I quickly grabbed a dishtowel off the counter and started on the floor.

"Have you been slacking on your exercises?" Jonathan's cold voice assaulted me. "And don't give me that crap about how many times you walk the dog. I've seen you carrying that mutt instead of forcing her to walk."

I obediently stopped what I was doing and met his eyes. "She wears out before I do."

"Then leave her in the yard while you get in your two to three miles. There's no excuse, Jessica. Those walks and the exercise DVDs I got you are supposed to be part of your everyday routine. We've had this discussion before; don't force me to have it again." He loomed over me, taking care not to step in the mess he'd created. When he drew back his hand, I lowered my eyes, prepared for the onslaught.

"Make sure everything is spotless," he snarled, walking away from me. "It doesn't matter how late I come in; I *will* check it." He opened the door to the garage. "And you really don't want me to find anything."

Chapter 15

Looking out across the kitchen and dining room, I wanted to cry. But didn't. I knew from experience it wouldn't make things better, wouldn't make *me* better. Instead, I tackled the job with the determination to do an excellent job while making quick work of it.

At least, that was my intention.

There wasn't an item in the kitchen that hadn't been affected by Jonathan's fury. I'd no idea how far the food could fly. The applesauce was especially difficult. It had gotten into every crack and crevice available—and many that weren't. Which meant that after getting the initial mess cleaned up, I had to go back over the entire kitchen, cleaning it from top to bottom, including spots on the ceiling that would later have to be touched up.

I thanked God Domino behaved for her bath. It made getting the bits and pieces of stuff still clinging to her fur a lot easier to wash away. With her wrapped in a comfy towel, I attended to myself, and then got all the laundry involved in the fiasco into the washer.

Finally able to relax—at least until Jonathan's return—I grabbed the phone and cuddled with Domino in a corner of the couch. Though I really needed to return Granny Ed's call, I had the sudden urge to speak with Daddy. And I knew exactly where he'd be at this time on a Monday evening.

"Thought I'd find you there."

He laughed. "Mayor or not, I'm still a teacher with responsibilities. How're you doing, sweetheart?"

I loved him far too much to tell him the truth. "Just sitting here with Domino. The question is how you're doing, Daddy. Mother seems concerned about the campaign."

"You know your mother. She thrives on these things." There was a hint of sadness in his voice.

"And you, Daddy? Are you really all right with the council's change in term limitations to get you back?"

"If it's what Bennington wants. And it's especially disconcerting with Franks vying for the seat. I'm not sure he's best for the community." He cleared his throat. "But you didn't call to talk politics, Jessie. What's up, sweetheart?"

I knew his question was sincere. I also knew the truth would break more than his heart. "I just wanted to hear your voice. It's been one of those days." I told him a highly edited version of my morning, omitting the session with Harris in its entirety.

"You know your grandmother, Jess. Sometimes she acts before she thinks. But she'd never do anything to deliberately hurt you."

"Yeah, I know." I also knew he was anxious to get back to grading exams. That's why it surprised me when he didn't.

"Now, Jessie, how are things going with Dr. Harris. I don't expect you to give me a blow-by-blow account of what you've been discussing," he quickly reassured me. "Just wanted to know if you like him and feel comfortable chatting with him."

"He's a nice man, Daddy. And he really likes you, which means a lot." I thanked him again for making arrangements for me to see Harris. He seemed pleased and satisfied with my answer, and after exchanging our traditional "I love you more," we hung up.

On to Granny Ed.

"I was beginning to wonder if I'd have to drive over there to check on you," she said, jumping directly into a conversation.

"Hello to you, too." I needed to keep my tone light, non-accusatory. "Jonathan asked me to let you know how awkward it is for him to take personal calls at work."

"The devil he did! He told you to make sure I never did it again. Bet he threatened to take away some of our Sunday time."

"Nothing about our Sundays," which was surprising. "But, yes, you're right. He doesn't want it to happen again. He's very particular about that. I'm not even allo-" I coughed to cover my mistake. "Sorry. I'm not supposed to call. It's all about appearances, Granny Ed."

"Whose? He's nothing but a stuffed shirt who's so full of himself he doesn't see anything beyond his nose." I pictured her usually smiling face creased in frowns. "I'm sorry, Jessie-girl, I shouldn't say such things. He really gets under my skin."

Was this the time? Could I ask her the question that had been burning inside me since her remark earlier that day about owning up to the abuse?

"Is it because he reminds you of Grandpa?"

"What the devil are you talking about? Your grandfather was the nicest, kindest man I've ever known! How, why," she seemed at a loss for words to my tentative question. "Nathan Collins and Jonathan Keller are further apart than night and day. For you to even think-"

"I'm sorry. It's just, well, neither you nor Mother have ever really talked about him. I, I didn't mean to upset you."

I heard her draw in a deep breath. "Your mother doesn't talk about him because she never got the opportunity to know him. She was only two when he died. I thought you," she stopped in mid-sentence. "This is about me saying you should tell your therapist about the abuse, isn't it?"

I gulped back my horror, managing to squeak a timid "Yes."

"Ah, honey, it's like me having Peter call you to the church this morning. I thought it would be good for you and Eric to see one another again. I didn't stop to think it would just upset both of you."

"I'm not sure I understand."

"Jonathan's so controlling, limiting your time with me, where you attend church, and such. After what you had to go through with your mother, it makes me so angry I could scream. If that's not abuse, I don't know what is!"

Now it was my turn to sigh—in relief. "You're right, he is," I agreed. "And, well, we're working on it. I mean, he's letting me go to the concert with you. That's a big step."

"It's a baby step." There was something there, something I couldn't quite put my finger on. She didn't give me any time to figure out what I might be missing. "Next Sunday we'll have a good long talk about Grandpa Nathan, sweetie pie. It's long overdue."

After making arrangements to pick her up for the Whitney's Connection concert, we said our goodbyes. It was nearly eleven, and Jonathan hadn't returned home. A small miracle in a day filled with one upset after another. When I finally settled in to sleep, I thanked God for getting me through the day.

And begged never to have another like it.

Chapter 16

I **didn't see** Jonathan at all Tuesday, neither had he left me one of his notes containing a long list of extra chores he expected to be completed by the time he came home. I'd like to think this was some sort of an apology, or contrition over the incident with the food. But Jonathan didn't do contrite. And I'd never heard him apologize for anything.

It was nice to have a quiet day, take care of my daily chores and spend quality time with my sweet little dog, who still seemed a bit jumpy.

As it neared 6:30, more than an hour past Jonathan's usual time to get home from work, I accepted this to mean he wouldn't be here for supper. I packaged the spaghetti and meatballs in the appropriate freezer container and tucked it away. One less meal to make in the future.

Late that night, or early the next morning, I heard Jonathan come in. He went through his dresser and closet banging things around, not a thought about me trying to sleep. Typical behavior on both our parts—I just lay there pretending to still be asleep. Even after all that had happened, I made certain his breakfast was ready as usual.

When Jonathan finally came down the stairs, he carried a suitcase and garment bag.

"I've decided to attend the conference after all. I'm leaving for Denver this afternoon and won't be back until Sunday evening. Might as well visit some old friends while I'm in the city." He set his things next to the door to the garage. "Please put my briefcase with the rest. I believe I left it in the office."

He didn't so much as glance at me. A reprieve? I'd no idea. I simply did as I was told before taking my place at the opposite end of the table.

"Just because I'm gone doesn't mean you can stay out to all hours, Jessica. You're to come home as soon as that concert is over. Don't think I won't know if you disobey. I don't have to use the phone to find out what you're up to."

The glance he gave me sent shivers down my spine. The thought he might have spies keeping an eye on me pushed his controlling behavior to a whole other level.

He nibbled at his breakfast, then left without another word. He'd never mentioned any conference, and it was rare for him to attend one. And though I felt his story wasn't the actual truth, it would've done no good to question him about it. As with his recent erratic conduct and what brought it about, if Jonathan didn't want me to know, I'd no other choice but to accept it.

Or did I?

Chapter 17

Claire left a short, enigmatic message on my answering machine while Domino and I were out for a walk.

"No time to talk now," she said, sounding out of breath. "This is my last day, so gotta get back to work. Just wanted to let you know you should be getting a surprise in the mail today or tomorrow. Love you!"

"What's Claire up to, Dom?" I patted her on the head, giggling when she darted off and returned seconds later with one of her soft, bouncy balls—something only played with when Jonathan wasn't around.

After a longer walk than usual, the game of fetch didn't last long. She curled up next to me on the couch, another thing that only happened when Jonathan was absent, and was soon asleep. With the contented sound of her breathing as a backdrop, I went through the mail I'd brought in earlier. Though I wasn't allowed to pay the bills, it was my responsibility to open everything and clip statements and return envelopes together, get rid of the junk mail, and save any ads that might interest Jonathan. It was rare to find something addressed to me, so it was especially nice to see the card from Claire. Obviously her "surprise."

And what a surprise! A pre-paid phone card so I could call her whenever I wanted. Now, instead of writing it down, I'd be able to *tell* her all about tonight's concert. What a treat!

The phone rang, startling me, though it didn't faze Domino at all. She simply rolled into a tight little ball and continued to snooze.

"I'm sorry not to call sooner," Granny Ed said after letting me know I'd have to meet her at the church instead of picking her up. "I knew they were going to have a meet 'n' greet for early birds but thought they had everything covered. Oh well, gives me the opportunity of saving us seats. This isn't a problem for you, is it, sweetheart?"

"Not at all. What about you? I know how much you hate driving after dark."

"Simple. You'll take me home after the concert. Listen," I could tell she'd moved the receiver away from her ear. It hadn't been necessary; the sounds of the guitars and keyboards were clearly audible.

"This is going to be so much fun!" With that gleeful statement, my eighty-year-old grandmother hung up.

~~~

The church was filled with so many people, I almost left. The elation I'd felt having this opportunity
~~~

of a more normal life—if only for this event—collapsed into a kind of claustrophobia. The overwhelming press of people and accompanying mish-mash of voices and noise took me by surprise. I'd never felt anything quite like this before, and wondered why such a reaction would suddenly appear.

Ushers urged people forward into the sanctuary, assuring them the concert would be broadcast on the screens placed throughout the area so they wouldn't miss a thing. I sank back against a wall in much the same way I would when shrinking away from Jonathan's wrath. That's when I spotted Paul Hillyard's face among the crowd. When he reached out for me, I astonished myself by latching onto his hand.

"I know I'm the last person you want to spend time with, Jess, but your grandma felt I'd be able to get through the mob easier than anyone else."

"You do stand out," I smiled, looking up into his soft hazel eyes. "What are you, six four or five?"

"Six, actually." He put an arm protectively around my shoulders when a group of teens rushed past, nearly bowling me over. "You okay?"

"Fine." I saw an opening to the right of the basement stairs and tugged him toward it, gripped by a sudden, intense need I didn't understand. "I know this isn't the best time to talk, but if you could just take a moment." I'd no idea what was happening, only knew what I felt.

Paul leaned forward, "You're sure you're okay?"

"I will be." I swallowed hard. "I-they told me how hard you worked to save Zach."

"If we'd gotten the call sooner, there might've been a chance," he shook his head. "I'm sorry."

"No, Paul," I said, clutching his arm. "*I'm* sorry. I should never have blamed you, never screamed at you as I did. I see that now." And I really did. A sudden epiphany. So sudden, I hadn't known those words would ever come out of my mouth. "Can you forgive me?"

He patted my hand. "I already did."

He gently turned me toward the stairs and said I should stay close. As he led me into the Fellowship Hall and to Granny Ed, I felt a burden had been lifted from my heart.

When he released my hand, he smiled widely, bent down and whispered, "Thank you, Jessie. That's a mighty gift."

For me, too.

Chapter 18

Inspirational, beautiful, moving. Everything you'd expect from a fundraising event to honor the victims of 9/11. Prayers were interwoven with some of Whitney's Connection best songs—most of which I'd never heard. Now and again, something familiar would grab my attention, but I didn't stop to think why. After all, I used to be Eric's sounding board.

Granny Ed and I held hands, cried, clapped, and exchanged smiles in the nearly ninety minute "service." The words and music slipped inside my heart, lifting my spirit in a way I hadn't felt since Zach's death. Now I knew why I'd had the unexpected urge to apologize to Paul. It was something about this place, this church, that brought out the best in me, of who I'd once been.

"...He's my Savior and my friend," the group sang. *"Who will love me till the end. As my sins are washed away, I know I'm finally here to stay."*

The words evoked a memory of Eric and I on a

picnic near Dover Creek. A warm summer's day when I sat on a blanket reading Eric's newest lyrics. When I jotted down a suggestion, he threw another rock into the creek.

I was jolted out of the memory by Granny Ed's voice.

"Go on, Jessie. Go on. They're waiting for you."

I looked up at the stage, suddenly aware that it wasn't just Eric and his band waiting for me to move, to go up front; so was the audience. I shook my head, pushed away my grandmother's hand, and attempted to ignore the voices of encouragement.

"Come on up here, Jessie," Bella Hillyard called. "It's time for you to sing some of those words you helped write."

"I didn't. Not really," I said, far to quietly for anyone to hear me. It didn't make any difference.

Eric Whitney stood in the aisle at the end of the row I was in. A lock of his dark hair swept across his forehead, and he smiled when our eyes locked.

Then he held out his hand.

~~~

I only have a vague recollection of what happened after that. Vague, yet in some ways more vivid than my everyday life. How is that possible?

I didn't really know what I was doing, had never been comfortable in front of audiences even when I sang with Eric's first band years before. I always stayed away from center stage, behind someone, if I could get away with it. The perfect place for a backing vocal.

Now, I took my place next to Bella and a woman I didn't know, as far from the mic as I could get. Eric had
~~~

chosen two songs from our past with lyrics I'd helped him with. I never actually wrote anything; it was more him bouncing ideas off me until he came up with what he really wanted.

Transported back to another time, another place, where confidence and belief in myself was bolstered by the love of my brother, Claire, and Eric, the music infused my soul. There was no tomorrow, no Jonathan, only the beautiful words we sang to a loving Savior.

Then it was over.

"Come out and see us Friday night at the old Moose Lodge on Graystone Road. We'll continue what we started here tonight, raising money for the victims, survivors, and those wonderful first responders of 9/11."

"It starts at 7:30," Bella added. "Bring your family and friends. We hope to see you there!"

When it was time to leave the stage. I'd intended to return to my seat, to Granny Ed, but my effort was thwarted by men determined to escort the entire band into a nearby classroom. My protest and concern for my grandmother resulted in Paul Hillyard rushing from the room. He returned a short time later with a very animated Granny Ed.

"Pastor said the donations far exceeded what we'd hoped for!" Her small round face was flushed with excitement. "This is a wonderful thing you folks have done."

Every attempt to encourage Granny Ed to leave was quashed. And once Pastor Nickerson joined us, I knew it was a losing battle.

Despite the exhilaration I felt from my brief participation and the success of the event, I couldn't help recalling Jonathan's intimation of my being watched. His threats weren't something to take lightly. And I certainly didn't want to end this remarkable day with a black cloud hanging over my head.

"We'd like you to sing with us Friday night." Eric and Bella smiled at me. "You did well tonight," Eric continued. "A great addition to the group."

"And we really want you," Bella said. "Besides, it's for a good cause. How can you say no?"

I was too stunned to speak, to think.

"Thank you, but," I shook my head in an effort to keep the darkness at bay. Fainting wasn't an option. "That's just not possible. I'm far too busy helping with the campaign."

"How about we leave it with Jessie promising to let you know tomorrow. Tonight's been a little overwhelming for all of us." Granny Ed grabbed onto my elbow. "She'll sleep on it. Right, Jessie-girl?"

Chapter 19

Granny Ed didn't stop talking the entire way to her condo. I wasn't sure she realized I'd barely said a word. She was so enchanted by everything that happened throughout the day, with Eric and Bella's offer to join the band Friday night the perfect finale. To her, anyway.

"That's so exciting, sweetheart," she turned toward me, her porch light causing her face to shine. "Surely you're not expected to attend your parents' fancy-schmancy dinner Friday evening."

"No, but-"

"But nothing, Jessie. You've always loved sing-"

"Not in front of a crowd."

"You've done some of your best work on a stage of one kind or another, and you know it. Why, without your input, Eric would still be floundering for the right words."

"Not true. And *you* know that's the truth. He's a

force to be reckoned with, always was. Too big for our little town."

She pooh-poohed my remark. "You make him sound so different, Jessie, not at all the way he really is. You were too young to understand why he had to leave, honey. Perhaps he didn't go about it the right way, but look at him now, how generous he's been donating his time. He didn't have to use the band's downtime like this. And, from what I've seen, it's something they all needed. Sometimes, success comes too quickly and involves leaving the ones you really care about behind."

"No. No. We're not having this conversation." As much as I loved and respected her, I had to put a stop to this before it went any further. There was too much at stake, too much to lose. Things Granny Ed must never know. "It's late, and I need to get home. I've a lot to do in the morning before that women's club luncheon tomorrow."

"I guess that's a night, then." There was a touch of sadness in her voice. She opened the car door and slowly got out. "You know, Jessie, everything happens for a reason. We might not have all the answers for what or why, but I believe God's got it all worked out. I also believe the first step in going forward is recognizing an opportunity to make needed changes when we're presented with one. I love you, Jessie Lynn. Thanks for the ride."

As she turned to go, I rolled down the window and called out, "I love you, too. Thank *you* for making sure I went to the concert. It was wonderful."

She didn't look back at me, just flicked a kind of backhanded wave before disappearing inside her condo. I hated our night ending this way, regretted bringing her down. But this lovely evening wasn't my life, no matter how much I might want it to be.

There were two messages on my answering machine when I got home. After letting Domino out, I reluctantly listened to them.

"Just found out from mom that you performed with Eric and the band tonight," Claire practically squealed. "I don't care how late it is, you call me! We need to talk!" Her enthusiasm was contagious as always, causing my mood to lighten.

For a second.

Jonathan's voice boomed across the room as I opened the door for Domino, stopping me in my tracks.

"That's one."

The machine clicked off as a shiver of apprehension made its way down my spine.

Domino pawed at my leg, reminding me she needed some attention after I'd been gone so long. Or maybe to say, "It's okay, I'm here."

Attending to my little dog helped distract me from the ominous message. Besides, Jonathan was attending a conference in Denver, more than a two-hour drive from here. He'd never come back just to...

No! This was my time. I'd already hurt my grandmother because intrusive thoughts about Jonathan's probable reaction to my performance tonight had tormented me. I was entitled to... To what?

I picked up Domino, grabbed the phone, and dialed Claire.

Happiness. I was entitled to be happy.

~~~

"Are you going to do it?" Claire asked. "You know
~~~

you want to, Jess."

"The old me, maybe," I admitted with a great deal of reluctance. "But I'm a long way from there, Claire-bear. It's a miracle I didn't faint. You know how nervous I've always been in front of a crowd."

"True, but you also enjoyed it. Tonight, too. I can hear it in your voice. It was good for you."

"Now you sound like Granny Ed."

"I'll take that as a compliment. Oof!" She moaned. "I think the little one's telling me it's time for bed."

"But you're all right?"

" 'Course, silly. We're both just ready to meet one another face-to-face." She giggled. "And Auntie Jess needs to make sure she gets to KC before this kiddo is old enough to vote!"

We talked awhile longer, making plans for my trip to see the baby—and Claire urging me to take Eric up on his offer. After nearly an hour and a half, we were both too tired to go on. With a promise to call again soon, I hung up, thrilled I'd had the chance to spend some quality time with my best friend.

By the time I got out of the shower, Domino was ready to go outside one last time before bed. I'd no sooner replaced the handset into the phone's base, when it rang. I laughed, positive it would be Claire with one last push to convince me to sing Friday night.

But my cheery hello was met with Jonathan's ice-cold voice.

"That's two."

Chapter 20

Jonathan's threat was like a challenge, daring me to get that third strike. And, in perhaps the most childish way possible, I accepted the dare, going in the opposite direction of anything he'd have allowed. No matter how stupid, insane, this seemed in light of Jonathan's penchant for abuse, once I'd made the decision to defy him, to sing with the band, my staunch determination to go through with it overruled all other thought.

The mutiny against him continued when I gave Bella Jonathan's fax number so she could send copies of songs they'd be performing. This added more to my list of infractions. By breaking the cardinal rule of staying out of his office and not using his equipment, the punishments that were likely to follow rose exponentially.

As I awaited the fax from Bella, I thought about what she'd told me regarding the upcoming concert.

"A couple of the participating churches have arranged for their praise teams to perform as well. Eric's still working out the details, but it looks like we'll have an opening act, then our set, followed by another group before we close. So, there won't be as many songs to learn. Well, you know what I mean. It will be good for the community and good for you as well." She laughed. "I'm guessing a little less stage time is a relief."

"I was trying not to think about it."

"Having second thoughts?"

"A few," I admitted. "But I'll be there."

"No later than 6:30." She reminded me before signing off.

The fax machine beeped, signaling an incoming message. By the time the long beep informed me the fax was finished, there were more than twelve pages of songs I needed to become familiar with. Glancing through them, I was thrilled to see most of them were on the CD Claire had given me. It would be a lot easier to learn the songs that way than trying to figure out the tune without the aid of an instrument. This was proving to be more overwhelming than I'd thought.

Of course, I hadn't given it much thought. After remaining awake all night, roaming about the house and watching mindless TV infomercials, the moment the clock hit seven, I was on the phone to Bella. Things snowballed from there.

No time to think about this now. I had to finish getting ready for the women's luncheon, and I dared not be late meeting Mother.

As I drove to the restaurant, I got the sudden, inexplicable fear that Jonathan had set a trap for me to fall into. He'd left the office unlocked, even sent me in to get his briefcase that morning before he'd gone to work. Not the norm at all.

Surely, not even Jonathan could devise such a devious scheme. He was controlling, easily angered, even vindictive, but capable of preplanning...

Offering up a form of temptation to use his computer and office equipment wasn't something I could fathom.

What about all those times he'd hurt me, *beat* me to the point he'd been forced to seek medical attention as far outside Bennington as he dared? Always sending me into the ER with explicit instructions on what to say and how to behave.

Except the last time when he'd no choice but have the ambulance come to the house. He'd gone too far that time. And I, like the fool I'd become these last four years, covered for him, for me, hating myself for my weakness while promising to forgive him for the unforgivable act.

All these things played over and over again in my brain without swaying my determination to keep my word to Eric and Bella—in spite, despite, what the consequences might be.

Would be.

If I allowed it. If, once again, I failed in my resolve to stand up to him.

The question remained as it always had: was I capable of stopping him once and for all?

I'd never been reckless, that had been more Zach's style than mine. Hopefully, this one time of throwing caution to the wind would not prove my undoing.

I put on my "game face" and joined my mother.

Chapter 21

I'd no idea my performance at the church the night before would be among the many discussions during the luncheon. Much to Mother's displeasure. She smiled through gritted teeth, and then proceeded as she always did, charming the women with her ready wit. It was only later in the parking lot that she let me know just how unhappy she was about my "stunt."

"Don't be fooled by that charlatan, Jessica. He's not the popular headliner he's led everyone to believe. Why do you think he's returned to his home turf?"

I shrugged my shoulders, ready to be done with this portion of the day. No, I didn't have a lot to look forward to, but at least it would be quieter than the last two hours.

"He said the band needed a rest," I answered. "They're donating their time-"

"So I've heard. He wants to be thought of as the musician with a golden heart, or some such nonsense.

That's just another of his lies. Another way to string people along into believing his garbage. One would think you had better things to do than stoop to his level." She glared down at me. "Don't embarrass your father and I, Jessica. It would be unwise on so many levels."

I'd been living with her threats my entire life. She may be formidable, but...

She wasn't Jonathan. He was on a whole other level than Ellen Randolph.

Other than the luncheon and my usual "scheduled" walks with Domino, I stayed home. I used the phone for a quick call to Granny Ed, so I could apologize for the way our night ended and then let her know I'd agreed to join the band for Friday night's concert.

"Good for you, Jessie Lynn. It's the right decision!" Her enthusiasm helped alleviate my fear of being in front of an audience again and really made me feel as though I *had* made the right choice.

As much as I wanted to share the news with Claire, it was best to wait until afterward to speak to her. The pre-paid card was great, but it still tied up the phone. Better to not risk missing another of Jonathan's attempts to check on me.

To be on the safe side, I made certain my daily chores were completed and added a special cleaning of his office. Even with as persnickety as he was, when I'd finished, the room looked far better than it would have if he'd cleaned it himself.

With help from the lyrics Bella sent, I sang along with the Whitney's Connection CD and quickly learned four of the songs—ones I remembered Eric writing shortly before he'd left town. There was a little stab at my heart when I realized he'd used pieces of poems I'd written for *Jesus My King* and *Gentle Savior*. I hadn't known, hadn't thought, he would take them and use them without getting my permission. This obvious plagiarism caused me to question Eric Whitney's overall honesty. I hadn't minded him using the alternate words I'd suggested as replacements for things he'd written, but these had been from *my* poems. The thought of having to confront him about this didn't thrill me. Neither did the knowledge he'd gone behind my back.

Early the next morning, Eric surprised me with a call. His voice was more business-like than friendly, bolstering my resolve to have a talk with him about the stolen lyrics. Though now wasn't the time.

"I think it would be best if you arrived at the venue at five. We'll have the sound check completed and will be able to run through the set. That okay with you?"

"Sure. I can use the practice." An understatement if ever there was one.

"We'll do a set of five songs, break for the local group On High, who'll be on about a half hour. Then we come back to the stage for a couple songs before the other acts join us for *God Bless America* and *America the Beautiful*."

I heard him whisper to someone but couldn't understand what he said.

"It'll be a great event, especially with the inclusion of the local bands. It's a good way to give them exposure outside their churches. Anyway, we'll see you at five." He hung up without saying goodbye or even asking if I had any questions.

It may have been six years since we'd been

together as a couple, but that didn't mean I couldn't tell something bothered him about tonight.

Had Mother actually acquired accurate information regarding trouble amongst the members of Whitney's Connection? I found myself praying she was wrong, that Eric's behavior had more to do with changes to the original plans for the night and nothing more.

And that he'd have a reasonable explanation for passing my work off as his.

Whatever happened, it would be an interesting night.

Chapter 22

It was an easy drive to the Moose Lodge. Traffic was light, lighter than I'd expected at this time of day. A good thing since the closer I got, the more nervous I became.

Practice went well, though Bella had to leave the stage several times because of "morning" sickness. Each time she dashed off to the restroom, Paul came out from behind his keyboards and raced after her. And they weren't the only ones who appeared preoccupied.

The other backing vocalist, Peg, was on her phone in between songs and more than a bit fidgety. The guy who played bass and the drummer seemed to be at odds with one another, all while Eric acted as if he was totally unaware of what happened around him. None of this helped the butterflies stirring in the pit of my stomach.

What the devil was going on?

"I'm not sure it's wise for Bella to perform

tonight." Paul strode to the edge of the stage. "She's never been this bad before."

"Oh, stop." Bella came up behind him and gave him a squeeze. "I shouldn't have eaten that pizza at lunch."

"You barely had a bite-"

"You just didn't see how much I ate." She winked at me. "You and Eric had your heads together the entire time. You both need to settle down and relax. The rest of you, too." She came up on the stage and stood with her hands on her hips, staring down her bandmates. "You act like this is the end of things, our swan song. For heaven's sake, I'm pregnant, not dying. It's not terminal. Just because things haven't been going as well as we'd hoped, doesn't mean it won't get better. We're down, but not out. So cut the gloom and doom guys, you're making us look bad in front of Jessie."

While everyone took their places, Bella came over and gave me a hug.

"It's not what it appears, Jessie," she whispered. "Sometimes people do stupid things for what they think is the right reason. They get caught up and out of whack when they get scared. Doesn't mean they're bad. You'll see."

She let me go and took her place between Peg and me. She flashed me a knowing grin, lifted her arm, and counted down, "Three, two, one."

Here to Stay was performed flawlessly, without the almost lackluster attempt before she'd gotten sick.

As I sang, her words ran through my head. *She knew what Eric had done.* I should've realized it the other night when she mentioned me singing the words I'd helped write.

I glanced at Eric, then over to where Paul sat at his keyboards. Was there *anyone* here I could trust?

~~~

Long before I got to the stage, the palms of my hands were soaked with perspiration, and the butterflies in my stomach seemed to have multiplied. The wonderful lyrics, some from my poems, carried me to a more peaceful, gentler time. *Saving Grace*, *Jesus My King*, and *Gentle Savior*, were all greeted with enthusiasm. And when we sang the final lines of *All He Has To Give*, the crowd rose to their feet, cheering.

For the first time in hours, Jonathan infiltrated my thoughts. I nearly tripped over Bella as we made our way to the room we'd been given backstage.

"Watch yourself," Paul said, catching me in time. "The performance make you a bit tipsy?" He let go of my arm and smiled. "It happens. Don't worry about it."

"You know," Eric sidled over to me, grinning like the proverbial Cheshire Cat. "Your voice is a real compliment to the group. It's sweet, clear, and sincere. What do you think, guys? Do you all agree Jessie's an asset?"

Sounds of approval rang out, causing me to wonder if this hadn't been part of the plan all along.

"Thanks," I said, trying to get heard over their overly enthusiastic words of agreement. "This has been fun. Scary, but fun. A one-time thing."

"Come on, Jess," Eric leaned in closer. "We need someone who won't just sing the words, but mean them. We're planning on sticking around the area for a while, to rest and regroup. Don't you think you could at least consider the offer before shooting us down?"
~~~

He was way too close, way to earnest. The smile I used to think of as charming now seemed manipulative.

Or maybe I was reading too much into it.

"You forget I'm married with responsibilities." Besides, if Jonathan even suspected I might consider such a proposal...

It wasn't something I wanted to think about.

Eric started to protest but stopped in mid-sentence as a firm hand clutched my elbow in that all-too-familiar way. I winced from the pain, not wanting to turn around, not wanting to face Jonathan's wrath.

"Wh-what are you doing here?" My voice shook as I cringed in preparation of his certain anger.

"I came to ask you the very same question, my dear." Jonathan spoke with such viciousness it shocked me. Especially since we weren't alone.

"If you people would excuse us," he addressed Eric. "My wife and I would like the use of this room for a few minutes. We need to have a discussion that can't wait until later."

Despite his silence, it was obvious Eric didn't appreciate Jonathan's curt dismissal of him and his band. No one moved, and if they didn't leave soon, things would only get worse.

"It's okay, guys. Really." I hoped my smile reassured them, even if it didn't have the same effect on me. "We'll only be a moment."

When Eric stepped toward Jonathan, Paul and Bella each caught hold of his arms and steered him out of the room. The others followed closely behind. When they'd gone, I shut the door and faced Jonathan.

The blow came so quickly, so powerfully, it knocked me to the floor. My cheek and jaw throbbed as tears stung my eyes. I stayed down, my eyes averted. Something inside him must have snapped for him to hit me in a place others could see. As his eyes bore through me, I'd never felt such intense fear.

"I hate you." His disgust permeated the small room. "I've known for a long time that I didn't like you but had no idea how much I truly hated you until now."

"Jon-"

"Shut-up!" His eyes flashed their fury as he raised his arm to strike me again. I winced in preparation for the blow, but it didn't come. I raised my eyes to find him on the other side of the room, intently peering out of the window into the darkness.

"Did you see us? Vickie and me?" He didn't look at me, nor did he await an answer. "The moment we met at the fundraiser, I knew she was special. She's sweet and funny—everything you're not. It's also a plus she doesn't have a neurotic mother I have to kowtow to." The derision in his voice was almost as damaging as his slaps.

"It didn't take much to convince her to have an affair. She saw how it was between us, and when I reached out to her, she was like putty in my hands. It's been perfect."

My involuntary gasp made him hesitate for a moment. He turned back to me, studying my reactions.

"Shocked that I would seek comfort from another woman? Don't be," he laughed. "She's not the first and won't be the last." He laughed again. "You've got to be the most stupid, ignorant person I've ever known. Do you honestly believe *you* could ever be enough to satisfy anyone? Look at your precious Eric. God meant more to him than you ever could, so he walked out on you just when you needed him most." His amusement at my expense made me realize how little I mattered to him. He leered at me, a triumphant gleam in his eyes. "Just like Zach."

Every fiber in my being rebelled. I stood, wanting to hurl myself at him, to attack and hurt him. But he was right, wasn't he?

How could I have believed Jonathan cared for anyone but himself? And that foolish belief that my sessions with Matt Harris somehow protected me from his wrath just proved his words about my stupidity.

"How's your face?" When he reached for me, I backed away.

"That wasn't the wisest move I've made, was it?" The sarcasm bit into my soul. "It's your own fault, you know. You should never have gone behind my back and done this. Whitney's a self-righteous fool and your association with him and his group makes you an even bigger one. How could you believe you'd get away with this, that I wouldn't find out?"

A knock on the door had me rushing toward it. Jonathan reached it first, informed the person we were busy, then slammed and locked the door.

When he finally looked at me, some of the fire had left his eyes, but the blankness reflected there seemed worse somehow.

"Whether we like it or not, Jessica, we're legally bound." His voice was flat, resigned, yet firm. "As much as we both may detest the arrangement, we shall continue as before. In other words, my darling wife, don't try suing for divorce. You won't get it—not even with that pretty little bruise on your cheek. You try to ruin me, you'll end up ruining your father. Then let's see him get re-elected. I'm sure Vern Franks could use your dysfunctional family to his advantage. The election's just a few weeks away, and Bennington's such a small town, the information would move quickly through the community."

"You'd do that, turn on my father after all he's done for you?" What was I saying? Of course he would. We meant nothing in the scheme of things.

"Not me, Jessica, *you*. It's all up to you what happens. As for me, I'll be made either way it goes. Vern is a generous guy, not the self-righteous hypocrite your old man is." He walked back to the window.

"You need to get this through your thick skull. I *own* you. One word, one more infraction, I *will* destroy your family. Let's start with your grandmother, shall we? A word here and there and she is no longer eccentric; she's a lunatic like your brother. Then we move to dear old dad. Not only will he never hold office again, he'll lose his prized teaching position. And your mother, the witch won't be able to show her face around here again." He turned to me, his evil expression palpable. "I have that power, Jessica. Be useful and compliant, and the status quo remains. Trust me, you don't want the alternative.

"Look, I'll drop cute little Vickie. Show you I'm sincere. Besides, she was becoming a bit too clingy. So, what do you say?"

What could I say? He was threatening my family.

Jonathan reached toward me, then dropped his hand, a sly smile on his face. When he opened the dressing room door, my breathing began to steady a little.

"I'm parked to the right of the building. If you

know what's good for you, care about keeping your family from disgrace, you'll meet me in the car in five minutes."

He left me then, thoroughly shaken. Try as I might, I couldn't think clearly. Just the idea of him trying to hurt my parents and Granny Ed was enough to keep me in line. He knew that, knew that no matter how much of a gulf had been between us, the Randolph family still had love on their side—even if it was buried under a mountain of garbage.

I had no choice but to obey Jonathan, and with tears of shame and defeat streaming down my cheeks, I quickly gathered my belongings. I pushed through the crowd enjoying intermission, rushing toward the entrance of the lodge, and praying I'd reach Jonathan's car in time.

I literally ran into Eric, mumbled an apology about being unable to continue the show, and attempted to move past him. He caught hold of my arm and forced me to face him. When he put a hand beneath my chin and turned my face into the light, I heard his breath catch in his throat.

Covering the bruise I was certain must be there, I jerked out of Eric's hands, then ran out of the building into the crisp night air.

We didn't speak on the way home, and once we reached it, all Jonathan said was that he'd make arrangements to retrieve my car in the morning. He left me in the living room and stomped up the stairs.

Alone with my thoughts, I fell completely apart. How could I have been duped into believing Jonathan ever loved me? No matter how hard I'd tried to live up to his demands, his standards, all he cared about was controlling me. I'd given my life to him, allowed myself to be mistreated because something inside me kept nagging that I deserved it. I never believed I had a choice, had just taken what was dished out and stuffed my own wants, needs, and personality into a past where I thought it belonged.

A past that was all tied up in Zach's suicide.

Tears streamed down my face as gut-wrenching sobs wracked my body. Matt Harris would be proud of me right now, I thought. I'd made a breakthrough on something I'd refused to talk about. Though I'd leaked some information that last session. Even then, I hadn't really told him anything.

I desperately needed someone to talk to. I didn't feel comfortable leaving a message with Harris's answering service. As for Claire, I couldn't drop this into her lap. Especially not over the phone. After all, she and Tommy were preparing for the birth of their baby.

I grabbed the handset and took it into the kitchen just as Domino raced down the stairs like she was being chased. I carefully picked her up, hoping Jonathan hadn't hurt her. I didn't put her down until I was satisfied she was all right.

Sinking onto one of the dinette chairs, I punched in my parents' number, hoping my father would answer. I didn't know what I'd say, just thought hearing his voice would help somehow. He didn't always approve of Jonathan, which was the one place where he and Mother butted heads. And though he'd never said it, I knew that deep down, he was sorry for the role he'd played in helping Mother get Jonathan and me together.

The phone rang five times before it was finally

picked up. With all the noise in the background, I knew their dinner party was still in full swing.

"Is anyone there?"

My mother's voice stabbed at me. Part of me wanted to hang up, but the larger part, the part that remembered the long ago warmth and comfort of her arms, that part won out.

"He, he hit me, Mother."

"What? Jessica, is that you?" The impatience in her voice was typical, the edge told me guests must be nearby.

"Jonathan hit me. My cheek's swollen and-"

I heard the intake of breath, the heavy sigh. "We can't do this right now, Jessica."

"Mother, please. Mama." A baby name I hadn't even thought to call her since I was little more than a toddler. How had it slipped out? How had I become so desperate?

"I've got to go now, Jessica. We'll talk later."

"No, please, no!" I screamed into the empty phone. I tossed the useless handset across the room and watched as it smashed against the refrigerator. Pieces of plastic, the battery cover, all skittered along the slick tiled floor, finally coming to a stop with a tiny click, click.

"Are You there, God? Are You listening? Because if you are, I need some answers. I need my life to change. I *need* a life."

Chapter 23

When Matt Harris called a little after five the next morning, I regretted the impulse of leaving a message with his answering service. I hadn't gone to bed, had fallen asleep with my head on the kitchen table, and was barely cognizant of my surroundings. But with Jonathan rustling around upstairs, I realized remaining on the phone wasn't an option. Despite his reluctance, I convinced Harris to meet me later at Wilton's Coffee Shoppe.

"At seven?" Harris asked, his voice filled with concern. "Are you sure you don't want to go to the office or meet earlier? I'm free till nine and am willing to-"

"It's great. Really." A click on the line signaled Jonathan lifted the receiver upstairs. "I'll see you then." I hung up quickly, not giving the doctor an opportunity to say another word. No need for Jonathan to know who'd called.

Unless he asked. Which I hoped he wouldn't.

I'd just dipped out pancake batter onto the griddle when Jonathan came into the kitchen. Early. By nearly a half hour. His ice blue eyes swept across the room, taking in my disheveled appearance, the mess I'd created throwing together his breakfast, and Domino's hasty exit. He didn't say anything, simply smirked when I reached up to my bruised cheek.

"I'd suggest a little extra make-up today since you'll have to run errands. Don't want any prying eyes or questions, do we?"

I shook my head, wondering if I was supposed to meet his gaze or keep mine downcast.

"I noticed the handset in the hall is missing. I've told you the thing won't properly charge if it's not kept in place between calls."

"It, um, there was an accident. It'll have to be replaced."

"Accident? Are you sure you didn't have a tantrum and throw it across the floor?" He drew closer to me. "I'd think very hard before you respond."

"I—yes, I threw it." I felt his hot breath on the back of my neck as he loomed over me. I tried not to shake, not to move.

"Better flip that pancake before it burns." Matter-of-fact? That wasn't one of his tones. "And you'll have to replace the phone and get groceries on your own." He tossed the keys to his car on the counter. "You'll need to use mine since yours won't be here till afternoon."

To Jonathan's delight, the sudden blare of a car horn made me jump.

"I'm going out and don't know when I'll be back.

You'd better be here when I return." He grabbed his weekend coat off the hook near the garage door before leaving through the front, smacking me on the rear as he walked past.

Once the door slammed, I ran to a nearby window to see who'd come to pick him up. It looked like Vickie Lassen from here, but I wasn't certain.

"Pretty bold, Jonathan," I mumbled. Domino gazed up at me, her little nose twitching. "The pancakes!"

Well, now they were cinders.

~~~

"Must've been quite a fall to cause that bruise." Matt Harris watched me over the top of his coffee cup. The din of all the people in the coffee shop, and the little nook we sat in, gave the illusion of privacy.

"I think we both know it wasn't a fall." I didn't avert my eyes from his. "No accident of any kind."

"Ah. You want to talk about it now?"

"I wanted to last night. Not so much today." I shifted my position and glanced away. "Can you tell me something?"

"If I can."

"If you live a lie long enough, does it somehow become the truth?" I shuddered at the thought, toying with my mug of hot chocolate. "I know it doesn't. Just sometimes feels like it."

Harris leaned slightly across the small table. "What are you trying so hard not to tell me, Jessie? What's so important you needed to call my service at two a.m.?"

"Accidents aren't always accidents. Nothing is ever what it appears." It's the closest I could come to revealing what caused the miscarriage.
~~~

Why was it so difficult for me to really talk to him, share with him? Why wouldn't the words come? "I'm sorry. This was a mistake."

"I don't think so." He rose at the same time I did. "What can I do to make you trust me?"

"I... I do trust you. I think." I slipped into my jacket. "Things just look differently in the dark." I held my hand out to him. "Thank you for meeting me. I truly appreciate it."

"That's it, then? You're going to walk away without an explanation? Jessie," his warm hand lingered on mine. "If someone was hurting my wife or daughter-"

"You're married with kids. Awesome." I pulled my hand from his. "And I took you away from them on a Saturday morning. I'm so very sor-"

"You're deflecting, Jessica. But, hey, I'll play along. Yes, I'm married with two daughters. Nine and seven. And each of them understands that when someone's hurting I need to be there to try and help them."

"Sometimes it's more important to consider others rather than yourself. Selfishness is a coward's way."

"And you're not a coward."

I shrugged. "I'd like to think I'm better than that. Not a hero by any stretch of the imagination. But not a coward."

"And neither am I, Jessie." Sadness flickered in his eyes. "I'm ready to help you with anything. Everything. It's not just my job; it's my calling."

His sincerity touched me deeply. "I believe you." But I still wanted to leave.

Something stopped me, urging that there was one

more thing he needed to know.

"I'll see you on Monday," I told him with a smile. "No more hiding. I promise."

At least, that was my prayer.

Chapter 24

After setting up the new phone and answering machine, I called Granny Ed to let her know how the benefit had gone. I breathed a sigh of relief when she didn't answer, left her a brief message, and told her we'd talk tomorrow. I'd barely hung up when the doorbell pierced the silence, startling both Domino and me. My inclination to ignore whoever it was lost to my hope the towing service had delivered my car.

I should've checked the peephole.

Eric Whitney didn't wait to be invited inside; he simply pushed past me into the living room.

Domino yelped fiercely at him, wagging her tail all the while. If she couldn't frighten an intruder, she'd make friends instead. Eric laughed at her silliness, petting her on the head as he scanned the room.

He lifted his eyebrows in a quizzical manner, frowned, and said, "He's not keeping you a prisoner. There are no bars on the windows, and you appear to have control of the doors, so what's keeping you here? I mean, you didn't answer the phone, so I thought maybe you were in chains or something."

"I think you should leave." I indicated the open door. It didn't faze him.

"Why? So you can allow that monster to smack you around some more? I don't understand how you could stay with someone who beats you."

The feel of his eyes on me, scrutinizing me, was unnerving. Bowing my head to avoid having to look into them, I slipped behind a chair near the entrance to the room. From here, I could watch him while remaining inaccessible.

"Do you feel safe there? No, don't answer me." He ran a hand across his head, ruffling his dark hair. "I'm not the one who tried to break your jaw, Jess. Remember? You have no reason to be afraid of me." He threw his hands in the air. "What happened to the intelligent, sensitive girl I used to know? She'd never have allowed herself to become someone's punching bag."

During my years with Jonathan, I'd found it did little good to defend my position—it was a lesson I'd learned well. Standing by and allowing myself to be berated for unknown reasons had been something I'd done as a child in the face of my mother's anger. Zach had been around then to run interference and make sure I was all right. When he was gone, I'd run to Eric and Claire for comfort. But that had been short-lived.

Now, I found myself biting my lips to keep from saying anything during his tirade, my anger and indignation from being confronted like this burning inside me. I wanted to escape, to run and hide, but he was standing in front of the chair, blocking my exit. I felt like a trapped and frightened animal. The only other choice was to face him.

"I'm not Jonathan's prisoner. I'm his wife." My voice shook, and I wanted to barf, but I met his eyes. "As with all marriages, we have problems-"

"Problems? Normal marriages have problems, Jessie. You're in the middle of a disaster!" He shook his head. "How can you be so calm? He hit you for singing with the group during a benefit concert. That's not a simple problem."

"I didn't say it was simple, Eric." Clearing my throat, I continued. "Not any more than what you did when you plagiarized my poems."

"You're comparing me to him?" When he reached for me, I scooted around the other side of the chair. He held up his hands and backed off. "How could you do that, Jess? We're nothing alike."

"The difference between the two of you is that I see him coming."

"I never hit you, hurt you."

"No, you just stole from me." I couldn't gauge the look on his face, didn't really care at the moment. "How dare you barge into my home and speak to me like this. You've got some nerve, Eric Whitney, to show up after all these years and think you know anything about me. One glimpse into my life and you have all the answers. Well, you don't. And I'd like you to leave."

He stood directly in front of me now. As he moved toward me, I shoved him with all my might.

"You keep your hands to yourself, Eric. You lost your right to touch me a long time ago." I struggled to keep tears at bay, to hold back the anger that wanted to spew out at him.

"Just trying to comfort you."

"No, you weren't. You're only here because you want something. Isn't that right? What's that envelope in your back pocket?" I walked toward him now with a new purpose in mind.

He didn't expect that.

"You wouldn't happen to have paperwork giving you my rights, would you? A little late, don't you think?"

"You don't understand-"

"Neither do you." I glared at him, trying to discern the look of confusion on his face. Suddenly, words to one of his first songs filled my mind. I didn't care what reaction he might have when I recited them.

"Time passes, setting the pace. Winners only win, when they choose to run the race." Forever Blue hung between us.

"So that's it, huh? You throw words I wrote in my face because I chose to pursue my dream?"

"No, Eric, because you took something that didn't belong to you to "win" your race."

"I needed the songs for the album. We scraped together everything we could to get it done in a cheap studio with a limited release."

My mother's words about him reverberated in my mind. "So things aren't going very well for you?"

He shook his head. "We're down now-"

"But not out. I heard Bella's pep talk. It doesn't change what you've done. Maybe if you'd thought to ask. But you didn't." I pointed toward the still open door. "Just go."

"Why won't you give me the opportunity to explain it to you?"

"Like you did before you left six years ago?" I shook my head. "Just leave the papers here, Eric, and get out."

"This isn't what I wanted, Jess."

"What more is there?"

"Divorce the jerk and join the group." He said vehemently. "Stop allowing him to use you."

What I wanted to say remained unsaid. Unlike the confidant musician he'd appeared to be the day before, he looked more defeated than I felt.

But that was something he'd have to deal with on his own.

ALICE K. ARENZ

Chapter 25

I leaned against the locked door, trying to catch my breath. I'd stood up to someone, fought for myself, for my rights. That was good, right?

Too bad it hadn't been Jonathan.

Loud voices in front of the house forced me back to the present. Jonathan. And Eric.

I flung open the door in time to find the two men inches from one another, both with fisted hands, neither looking to back away from a fight.

"If you come here again, Whitney, I'll get a restraining order!"

"Go ahead and do that and I'll make sure the cops know what you did to her last night. One look at her face, and it'll be apparent which one of us should have that order."

"Why you son of a-"

"Stop!" I shouted, stepping onto the porch and peering at the houses next to us, praying no one watched behind closed doors. "Eric was about to leave, Jonathan. He realized he had no business here."

"Really? After how long? Exactly how did you entertain-"

"Get your mind out of the gutter, Keller. You-"

"Shut up! Both of you." I didn't shout, kept my voice low, stern. "Get out of here, Eric." I could tell he was reluctant to do so with Jonathan glaring at me. But I held my ground. "Go." I went back inside, refusing to get involved any further.

Domino bounced at my heels as I made my way to the kitchen, all the while praying the men would somehow disappear. Or, at the very least, give up their macho acts and go their separate ways. Whatever happened, one thing was certain: sooner or later, I'd have to deal with Jonathan.

It was Saturday, the one day he allowed himself more than one cup of coffee. He hadn't had anything from the pot I'd made for his breakfast, and though it was still full, I wondered if perhaps I should make a new one.

I'd picked up the pot when the phone rang. I grabbed the receiver from the wall phone and had it wrenched out of my hand. Jonathan slammed it back into place so hard, I wondered if I'd have to replace that phone next.

"What do you think you're doing?" He growled.

"Making you a fresh pot of coffee and the ph-"

"Don't play coy, Jessica," he sneered. "Doesn't work for you." He loomed over me, forcing me back against the sink. With a swipe of his hand, the glass coffee pot flew from my grasp, shattering as it landed onto the porcelain. Jonathan grabbed my arms in an iron grip that made me wince. "What did he want?"

"Nothing," I said, trying not to cry.

"It's not enough I have to be under a microscope because of that shrink your father set you up with, now your old boyfriend's got you thinking you can run off and sing in his band." His pale blue eyes were like marbles frozen in the snow, his face rigid as stone.

He let go of me, and I ran into the living room. He caught me by my hair, yanked hard, then released me so suddenly I fell backwards. My hands flailed behind me, searching, and finally catching the arm of a chair in time to keep me from landing on the fireplace hearth. He made no attempt to help me, simply stood there staring.

"Shall we try this again? What did he want?" Disgust permeated from him, which is why I was surprised to see him take a step back and place his hands into his pockets.

"He-he wants me to sign paperwork giving him rights to some old poems."

"Excuse me?"

"They're just some poems I wrote a long time-"

"You expect me to believe that crap?" He snorted. Then, with an evil grin, "He ripped you off, didn't he?"

I didn't answer. Didn't need to.

"Where're my keys?" He nodded when I pointed toward the entryway. "Don't forget what I said last night about your family, Jessica. Franks is ahead in the polls right now, not by much, but enough. If you defy me, I'll see to it Vern Franks is the next mayor of Bennington. And that's a promise you can count on."

Not long after Jonathan's departure, the tow service brought my car home. After the driver left, I stood in the doorway, staring at my vehicle, thankful I had a means of escape.

What an odd thought.

Domino yipped at me from just inside the house.

"What's up, Dom? Huh, little sweetie?" I picked her up, grabbed my keys, and together we checked to make sure everything inside the car was where it was supposed to be. Even the bright yellow coat. Satisfied nothing was missing, I figured addressing the mess in the kitchen should be next on my agenda.

"Just like last time," I mused, picking up shards of glass. "He causes havoc, then walks away to make me pick up the pieces. Literally."

Chapter 26

I lost track of time. If it hadn't been for the cast of shadows against the living room walls, I wouldn't have realized afternoon was waning. I didn't know how long Domino and I had been on the couch, couldn't remember grabbing the new phone before sitting down. But the handset was in my lap, waiting to be used. A glance at my watch said it was a little after three. Why did it feel so much later?

Simple, really. I hadn't slept the night before.

The phone rang, and, believing it would be Granny Ed, I answered it—totally unprepared to find Bella on the other end of the line.

"Please don't hang up, Jessie," she pleaded. "I'm responsible for using your poems."

"I don't need this, Bella. I told Eric I'd sign the papers, so let it go."

Hanging up on Bella Hillyard wasn't that easy. No, I didn't have to pick up when she called back;

something told me I should.

"Eric had the music but no lyrics." Bella's story was a convoluted one that included a major betrayal by a manager or something, missing money, bills that needed to be paid, and a lot of terms I wasn't familiar with.

I wanted to tell her I didn't care, that they'd get what they wanted, and then hang up. Again. I didn't need the train wreck of their lives; I had enough to deal with in my own. So, why couldn't I just cut her off, make sure she knew never to call again? Her pain reeled me in, forced me to listen. And for reasons I didn't understand, made me want to help.

"I'd found this ragged notebook of poetry in one of Eric's bags. Okay, to be honest," she gave a nervous laugh. "I knew it was there because he carried it everywhere. I wanted to know what it was, so..."

A memory flashed of me handing the notebook filled with bits and pieces of poetry to Eric. After Zach's death, I'd no desire to ever write in that book again. Eric had fished it out of the trash, tried to get me to put it someplace for safekeeping. Instead, I'd given it to him, told him to take it away, to *keep* it. So, in essence, the poems belonged to him.

Still, it would have been nice if he'd asked...

If it hadn't been for the sound of her breathing, I wouldn't have known she was still on the line. I remained quiet, waiting for her to continue, but hoping she'd hang up instead.

"The words and music matched, were meant to be together." She finally said.

"Bella-"

"I didn't realize they were yours. The initials were

L. Z."

"Lynn Zachary." I whispered. "A sort of pen name." Something Zach and I made up so very long ago. A ruse to keep my love of writing from Mother. I'd kept the notebook in a special place in his room.

"Sometimes," Bella continued softly, "it's better to ask forgiveness afterward instead of letting an opportunity slip by while you're seeking permission."

"I gave the notebook to Eric. If he hadn't taken it when he did, it would've been destroyed years ago. It was his to do with what he wanted." The pounding in my head made it difficult to concentrate. I desperately needed food and Tylenol. Not necessarily in that order. "None of you did anything wrong. I'll sign the paperwork and make it official."

She expressed her relief with a huge sigh. "Thank you for being so gracious, Jessie. We, well, we'll be in Allentown for the next few weeks." She gave me her parents' address as well as that of the motel where the rest of the band was staying. "We've got a concert tonight at Hopewell Church. We'd love if you'd join us. It starts at eight."

That was my cue to finally hang up.

Chapter 27

I downed the medicine for my headache, dished out some treats for Domino, and made myself a turkey and Swiss cheese sandwich. I hadn't been at the table long when Mother stormed into the house. And from the look on her face, I figured Jonathan had spoken with her.

I gazed up at my mother, admiring her poise and the beauty she still possessed. Zach's illness had been hard on her, but she'd always bounced back—kind of like Zach. Until that last time. Even if she never admitted it, I knew Granny Ed had been responsible for pulling her out of the alcoholic haze where Mother had landed after Zach died. They may not like one another, but Granny Ed loved her daughter enough to save her life.

Right now, Mother's eyes were a pool of grey fire surrounded by thick lashes and brows that slashed across a forehead wrinkled in anger. She stood before me like a volcano ready to erupt. I braced myself both physically and mentally for the fire to spew from her mouth and rain down upon me.

"What, in all that's holy, has gotten into you, Jessica?" The torrent had begun, and I knew there was no way to stop it. "You've got to be out of your mind to have taken up with the likes of Eric Whitney. I don't know how many times I've warned you about him. And I don't care if he's found religion and is selling it on the mountaintops. That boy's never been any good, running off the way he did without telling his folks proved it. The moment that band came to Bennington, Jonathan saw the change in you. He knew what might happen. Warned us. But for you to actually go behind our backs as you have, gallivanting around like you're some kind of rock star," she pointed a long finger at me. "Then having an affair-"

I'd never laughed in the face of my mother's anger, never had the courage to oppose her in any way. But I laughed now, heartily. It shocked her, caused her to stop the bombardment and stand staring at me aghast.

"Have you gone mad?" She was so completely bewildered by my behavior, I decided to take advantage of the situation.

"You're *my* mother, yet you believe everything Jonathan says about me. You treat me like I'm the in-law."

I knew she wouldn't deny it. Jonathan had been her pet the moment she'd "discovered" him and brought him home. In her eyes, he could do no wrong. From the perfect way our names fit together—Jonathan and Jessica Keller—to the fact that she'd handpicked the man himself. If there was something wrong with our marriage, you could be sure I was to blame.

"Have you ever thought about really listening to me? To actually hear what I've tried telling you?"

"Do you have any idea how this sordid affair will play in the press?"

"Jonathan's affair, Mother. To Vickie Lassen. He even took her to the benefit at the Moose Lodge last night."

"Vern Franks's popularity has been creeping up in the polls," she went on, ignoring what I'd said. "People are starting to believe his hype. With you seeing that shrink and strutting about with another man-"

"You're not listening. Just like you wouldn't listen when Zach asked for help." That got her. She reached behind her until she connected with the back of a chair. I pulled it out for her, and she sank into it, barely missing Domino.

"How dare you-"

"Tell the truth? Stop denying it? Daddy finally accepted it, Mother, why can't you?"

"You are not going to turn the topic of this conversation to your brother. He has nothing to do with any of this."

"He does, though." Tears streamed unbidden down my face. Not for myself, for her. For the woman whose hope in the future died with my brother.

She reached inside her purse and withdrew her gold cigarette case. She wouldn't light it, but it didn't keep her from putting a cigarette into her mouth.

She struck a comic figure, sitting there in all her finery with that noxious weed hanging from her lips. Yet, somehow, I couldn't bring myself to laugh at her again. Instead, I removed the cigarette from her mouth and knelt in front of her.

"You don't need these, Mama." I set the case on the table and took her hands in mine. "What you need is to talk to someone like Matt Harris."

"No. No." She shook her head and tried to pull from my grasp.

"Yes, you do. It's funny, I didn't really tell him anything. I only kept the appointments because of Daddy, but it helped somehow. Dr. Harris never judged, never criticized, even when I quizzed him over and over about his own life. What I should have done, wish I'd done, was really talk to him."

"So?" She reclaimed her hands, rubbing them as if I'd hurt her.

"I don't know." I shrugged my shoulders and stood. "I'm waiting for God to show me the answers."

"God," she huffed. "Even if He does exist, He doesn't care. If He did…"

"Zach would still be alive." I finished for her. "Maybe. But that was *his* choice, wasn't it?"

"If you or Peter Nickerson had told us what was going on, Zach would still be here."

I shook my head and walked over to the baker's rack where Zach's graduation photo sat. I looked at his smiling face and detected something I hadn't seen before. There was an oddness to his eyes…

"Did he rape you?" The words were so quiet, so soft, I almost thought I'd imagined them.

I turned back to my mother, the earnest look on her face etched itself into my heart.

"Yes. If I'm completely honest, I'd say he's been doing it as long as we've been married."

"Oh!" A well-manicured hand clutched at her

throat. "And that bruise isn't from falling?"

"No. It's my reward for singing with Eric's group last night."

"Is it… Is it true about the affair, Jessie?" The use of my nickname nearly did me in. I swallowed hard and shook my head.

"Not me. Jonathan."

She nodded, apparently satisfied with my answer. She straightened her shoulders, drew in a deep breath, and stood.

"So where do you go from here?"

"Escape, maybe?" I smirked. "I'm not sure. Like I said, I'm waiting to hear from God. But, Mother, there's something you need to know before you go. Jonathan threatened to ruin our family if I acted against him. I'm pretty sure he's been feeding Vern Franks information. I don't know what kind, or how it could work against Daddy, but knowing Jonathan..."

She patted my shoulder, dug into her purse, and pulled out her cell phone. "That might come in handy," she handed it to me. "If you decide to... get away for a while." She reached back inside her purse and withdrew the charger. "Keep it close, Jessie. And don't worry about your father. Franks isn't half the man he is and this town knows it."

When she left, I watched until she got into her car. I closed the door and stood for a moment with my back against it, listening as my mother drove off.

Maybe...

I lost little time dialing information for the number of Hopewell Church in Allentown. All the church secretary told me was what I already knew: Whitney's Connection was scheduled to play at eight.

I tried the numbers I had for Eric and Bella, but neither of them picked up their phones.

"I've got a decision to make now, Dom," I said, more than a little frustrated. I lifted my faithful friend, hugging her till she wriggled to be set free.

It had been a long time since I'd knelt to pray, but I did so now. As Domino climbed aboard the back of my legs, I begged God to show me a sign.

Chapter 28

The phone rang while I was in the midst of my prayers, and, rather than answer it, I continued to entreat God for help with my dilemma, an unmistakable sign one way or another. Whether it was meant that way or not, Eric's message on the answering machine seemed too coincidental not to be the sign I'd prayed for.

I tried returning his call to no avail. After three tries, I finally left a message that I was on my way to join the group in Allentown.

Running upstairs, with Domino trailing after me, I ran on auto-pilot, not really thinking about what I was about to do. I tugged my overnight case down from a closet shelf and started throwing things into it. I checked through the few dresses I thought would be appropriate, selected a simple black linen with a tailored look, and pulled out my black flats to go with it. It wasn't long before I was ready to leave.

Domino watched with expectant eyes as I headed for the garage. I hung the dress in the backseat, then threw my case into the trunk next to the old picnic hamper Granny Ed had given me several weeks ago. The bright yellow parka from All Weather Gear peeked out from beneath my overnight case. I reached for it, considered tossing it out, but decided to let it remain where it'd been since Granny gave it to me in September.

Domino followed me into the house, yipped when I took my jacket from the hall closet, and ran to where her leash hung near the front door.

"No time for a walk today, Dom," I told her. "Do you need to go out before we leave?" She ran to the back door and jumped up and down until I opened it for her. I couldn't leave her behind. The thought of what Jonathan might do to her made me shiver.

Domino ran up the steps and bounded inside as I filled a zippered food bag with her food. I grabbed several packets of treats and plastic bowls suitable for food and water. After closing and locking the back door, I looked around the kitchen one last time before shutting off the light.

Back in the garage, I let my small dog into the backseat, then climbed in behind the steering wheel. Taking a deep, fortifying breath, I started the car, noted I had a full tank of gas—or close to it—and, as I let the engine warm, turned on the radio.

"Once again," the announcer said. "There is a travel advisory out for the Bennington, Allentown areas. Those sprinkles may not look like much now, folks, but the National Weather Service is expecting temperatures to drop-"

I shut off the radio and pulled out of the garage. The route around the mountain would take longer, and with a storm coming, there'd be more traffic, which could make the drive even longer. It wasn't raining here, so maybe I could beat the storm entirely by taking the more direct route over the mountain. The road was often closed by this time of year, but since the weather had been exceptionally mild, I was certain it would be open.

There were no barriers on the highway, no signs warning of imminent closure. This was not only reassuring but made me feel as though it were an omen of good things to come. As I started climbing the mountain highway, light rain dotted my windshield, but I wasn't concerned. It wasn't until I was forced to switch the defroster on high to keep ice from forming on the windshield that I began to worry. And by the time the snow flurries began, I knew that my best bet was to continue pushing on and pray it wouldn't amount to much. When it changed from flurries to white-out conditions, I knew I was in trouble.

My speed was slow but steady. With no one in front or behind me, and visibility down to what was directly before the car, it was dangerous to keep on going. I searched my memory, trying to recall if I was near any turn-outs, while my eyes were trained on what had become a grey wall in front of me. Once in a while the wind would scatter the snow from the pavement to let me know I was still on the highway. But those moments were getting fewer and farther between.

"It looks like we're going to have to stop for a while, Dom." My little dog gave a light bark in response to my voice.

I stopped the car, leaving the headlights on for a few minutes. The light bounced off the snowfall and reflected back to me. Before I shut off the car, I checked Mother's cell phone. The words assaulted me in much the same way as Jonathan might; no service.

The digital read-out faded, leaving the car in a kind of surreal light. I pulled my jacket closed, zipped it shut, and tugged a pair of gloves from the pockets. I slipped the one-size-fits-all stretch acrylic gloves over fingers that were already growing stiff.

I looked behind me at the 60/40 backseat, wondering how difficult it would be to climb back there. And once there, would I be able to fold part of the seat down and tug the box and basket that was full of Granny Ed's emergency kit to where I could go through them?

It had been a long day, and it was clear it was going to be even longer. If I waited, the snow would just get deeper and the cold would creep inside the car and make it unbearable. I needed the parka and boots now.

First things first.

Like an expert contortionist, I turned and twisted until I was able to pull the latch that would release the smaller side of the backseat so it could fold down. No matter what I did, however, it didn't cooperate.

"Oh, be that way!" My comment received another sharp yip from Domino. I turned around, stroked her head and cooed at her, hoping it would be enough to reassure her everything would be all right.

I pocketed my keys before opening the door and flipping the lever to open the trunk. I took a deep breath of the rapidly cooling air and braced myself.

"Be right back, Dom."

The snow piled into my sneakers as I made my way around the car. Icy pellets stung my face and clung to my lashes. It seemed the more rapidly I blinked, the more ice built up, weighing the lashes down and making it even more difficult to see. Shivering, I opened the trunk and yanked on the bright yellow parka until it came free of my overnight case. I slipped it in on then pushed at the seat back until it finally tumbled forward.

My feet were wet and getting colder by the second. I needed to move quickly.

I pulled the small box of extras from Granny Ed's list out of the way so I could shove the old picnic hamper through the opening to the backseat. It wasn't as easy a task as I'd hoped because the bottom of the old wooden basket kept catching on the trunk's carpet. When it finally broke free, I called out in celebration. The sound of my voice fell eerily flat in the claustrophobic whiteness. There was no echo, no depth. No life. This time when I shivered, it was as much in fear as it was from the cold.

Domino's little black and white face peered out from the backseat. The little puffs of smoke from her breath got me moving again. I shoved my overnight case toward the opening, grabbed the small box containing the rest of the survival kit, as well as the shovel, then closed the trunk. As I returned to the driver's door, I ran through the list of items my grandmother had insisted were part of a well-stocked kit. The one thing it lacked was the thing I needed the most.

Courage.

Chapter 29

Clearing frost from the windshield, I realized it finally stopped snowing. The eerie whistling from the wind trying to penetrate the car had also ceased. I looked out at the glistening whiteness as it sparkled in the dim light reflected from inside the car.

I remembered a Christmas card that depicted a full moon shining down on a wonderland of bobsleds, horse-drawn sleighs, and beautifully decorated trees; a scene from an idyllic past designed to spur one's imagination and warm the heart. But the memory was in sharp contrast to my reality: I was trapped halfway down a mountain road, miles from civilization, with no way to call for help.

"Stupid! Stupid!" My voice was harsh against the silence surrounding me and was rewarded with a piercing bark from the backseat.

"Sorry, girl." I turned to see my little dog shivering among the folds of her favorite car blanket. Her large, dark eyes peered at me anxiously as I patted my lap.

"Come here, Domino. We'll warm one another up."

With a plaintive whine, she left her blanket, jumped to the console, then settled on my lap. I stroked her soft fur with what I hoped she'd perceive as reassurance but was sure she wasn't fooled. Still, as she cozied up against me, her shivering stopped.

The candle in the tin can lit the interior of the car with a flickering light that may have been considered romantic under different circumstances. The very thought of romance in any context left a bitter taste in my mouth. I quickly swept it from my mind and concentrated, instead, on the small amount of warmth that came with the candlelight.

My muscles and joints were beginning to stiffen, making me wish I'd been able to figure out a way to get into the long johns and sweaters Granny Ed had given me. Still, I'd thanked God repeatedly for my grandmother's insomnia, the TV program she'd seen about being prepared for winter emergencies, and the stubborn streak and love that caused her to get all these things for me. I might not be warm, but I wasn't nearly as cold as I'd have been without the parka and fur-lined snow boots.

An involuntary cold chill ran the length of my spine. I tugged at the insulated blanket that had fallen from my shoulders, my jerky movements unsettling Domino so much she returned to her own blanket in back. I turned to her, and the sad look on her little face had me close to tears.

The urge to cry, to break into torrents and spasms of self-indulgent tears was strong. But giving into such emotions could only damage and defeat what little fight I had in me. It was then I remembered the courage and determination of the heroes of 9/11. My plight was nothing in comparison to theirs—a good reminder in the face of adversity.

I pulled my left arm from beneath the blanket, tugged at the sleeve of the parka, and leaned forward to look at my watch. The glow-in-the-dark hands caught the candlelight and winked up at me.

Midnight: time again to start the car.

When I'd decided my course of action about running the car, I knew I'd also need to remember to keep the accumulation of snow around the tailpipe cleared. I'd been out several times to check the pipe, assuring myself it was clear enough for the exhaust to float away from the car. It almost seemed a dichotomy, starting the car to run the heater but having to go out into the cold each time to make sure it was safe to run the car in the first place. Still, it was better than the possible alternative.

I pulled both the quilt from my original emergency gear and the stadium blanket from Granny Ed around my neck, watching the expanding ghosts as the windshield defrosted. The little red lights on the dashboard were a reassuring sign of civilization but were only a temporary comfort.

The needle on the fuel gauge pointed to slightly under half a tank. With a heavy sigh, I snuffed the candle and sat back to enjoy the growing warmth issuing from the heater vents.

When Domino gave a quiet whine, I reached back to pet her and pulled her blanket closer around her. She lay there shaking, her limpid brown eyes watching my every move.

"I know you're uncomfortable, Dom. Hungry, too, I'll bet. I know I am." I'd only had a bite of the sandwich I'd made before Mother barged into the house. Before that...

I thought about the granola bars in the basket but didn't feel like having to dig for them. I'd manage. And knowing my dog, she would have been snacking on her food throughout the day. We'd be all right a few more hours.

When the warmth from the heater began to seep into my bones, it was a sign to turn off the car once again.

Past time according to the car's clock.

"Darn!" I brushed at tears rolling down my cheeks in spite of my determination not to cry, shut off the engine, and relit the candle.

The sudden silence was deafening. I wished for the return of the wind and the sound it made as it blew through the trees and whistled around the car. Then, there'd be some sense of being, some acknowledgment of the world outside the confines of the vehicle. Instead, we were left with the intricate sounds of silence resounding in our ears. Proof, beyond a shadow of a doubt, that we were utterly alone.

There was no way to gauge time beyond continually checking my watch. Not such a good idea when each second seemed hours long. In the beginning, I'd been able to estimate what to do from how long it took the windshield to fog over before starting to freeze after shutting off the car. As it grew later and the temperature dropped, the ice kept creeping further and further across the windshield, leaving only the small patch in front of me where the heater melted it each time.

"I wonder how deep it is out there."

Domino barked sharply in response, causing me to realize I'd broken the barrier of silence by speaking my thoughts aloud.

"Sorry, girl. Didn't mean to startle you." Guess the quiet and close quarters were getting to me. One thing was certain: if I didn't get out long enough to stretch my legs, I would soon go stiff. And with the cold setting in, I was afraid if I didn't move, I'd remain frozen in my current position.

I pushed the front seat as far back as it could go, rubbed my aching limbs, and glanced out the window. One way or another, I'd get into those long johns.

It took awhile, a lot of twisting my body into positions I never would've thought possible, but I got them on—over the top of my jeans. It wasn't pretty, but it worked. Afterward, I tugged on the oversized sweaters Granny Ed had given me. The down parka slipped over the top without being too tight, something that really surprised me.

The moon's gentle light shone down upon the shimmering expanse before me, adding a beauty to my surroundings that offered a strange sense of security. During the white-out, I'd been claustrophobic and close to a panic attack. But once the snow stopped and the clouds moved away from the moon, I'd begun to feel calmer and more hopeful.

The enormous pines nearby danced in front of the moon, playing a game of hide and seek as they shifted in a sudden gust of wind. It left as quickly as it came, with a whoosh that echoed around the car.

I will not be afraid. I will not be afraid.

If I kept repeating the phrase, would it sink in and actually have the power to transform me?

I wanted an answer, needed one, but was too terrified to wait for that still small voice to speak. Waiting was silence and inaction. I'd already spent too much of my life that way.

Searching the small box containing pieces of my survival kit, I grabbed one of the flashlights and prepared to go outside. But when I flipped the switch, nothing happened.

Don't panic, Jessie. Think.

The batteries had been installed wrong. I rearranged them, screwed the base back into place, and turned it on. It worked.

"Thank you, God." I whispered.

I glanced back at Domino huddled amidst the folds of her blanket. Her eyes were closed, and her deep, even breathing said she was asleep. Satisfied she'd be all right, I pulled up the hood of the parka, wrapped my scarf around the lower part of my face, and shoved at the car door until it finally opened enough to allow me to get out.

Snow piled into my mid-calf boots sending an instant chill through my legs and ankles despite the protection of my jeans and long johns. I looked about me, astounded by the accumulation of snow.

"At least a foot if not more!"

I stomped my feet and jumped around in an attempt to warm myself as well as get in a good stretch before taking the shovel out of the trunk again. While I dug out the area around the driver's side—front and back—the howl of a coyote caught my attention. I stopped to listen to the mournful cry as it broke the stillness of the night, echoing eerily through the mountains and back again to its point of origin.

My overactive imagination had me shining the flashlight all around me, searching the shadows, and wondering just how close the animal might be.

Could it be one of the wild dogs Gavin Hardesty had spoken about at Daddy's campaign fundraiser? He'd said they were "rabid as wolves," which didn't make much sense. Not all wolves were rabid.

Stop, I told myself sternly. This line of thought would get me nowhere.

I checked on the tailpipe, relieved the snowpack appeared far enough away not to be of concern. Still, while I was out, might as well scoop out the area a little more to be on the safe side. That accomplished, a few more shovelfuls further away from the car would give us a spot to relieve ourselves.

It took longer to convince Domino to come out of the car than for her to do her business and return to her blanket. She wasn't thrilled when I lifted her over the front seat, so I could rearrange the basket and my overnight case in order to relatch the seat. There would be a little more insulation between us and the outside with back up. Once I'd accomplished my mission, Domino gratefully returned to her blanket.

There'd be more room to stretch out in the passenger seat, and since I wasn't about to try to dig that side out, I'd no choice but to climb over the console to get there. I prepared myself for yet another acrobatic adventure. I pulled the driver's door shut, snuffed the candle, and moved the coffee can to the floor before struggling to my destination. All the extra clothing might keep me warmer, but it made maneuvering in a tight space a bit challenging. By the time I was comfortably ensconced in the passenger seat, a trickle of perspiration made a slow descent down my spine.

But it didn't keep me from starting the car.

Pulling my blankets over me, I laid the seat back and snuggled down to enjoy the warmth issuing from the vents. I promised to be more careful this time, to shut off the car when I was supposed to. But when the clock on the dash told me time was up, I couldn't bring myself to do it. All I wanted was the chance to get the chill out of my bones, wait a little longer.

As a precaution, I cracked the driver's window then hunched into the seat. I knew it wouldn't take long now. It was only a matter of a few more minutes, and I'd be warm...

Chapter 30

My fingers and toes ached, and every breath I took made my lungs burn. I awoke disoriented, trying to get my bearings. It wasn't the most pleasant way to awaken, but at least both Domino and I were still alive.

And it was morning. The brilliance of the sun in a cloudless blue sky shined through the windshield, glinting off the crackled ice, bringing a ray of hope. It also showed me there was even more snow on the hood than had been there when I'd gone to sleep earlier that morning.

The car wasn't running, and there were no lights on the dashboard. I'd either run out of gas or lost the battery. Neither prospect boded well.

Mustn't panic, mustn't panic.

I moved the seat to a more upright position, wondering what I should do. Domino jumped into my lap and whined softly.

"Sorry, girl. I should never have gotten you into

this mess." It was bad enough I'd allowed myself to get into this situation, but to have involved my innocent dog...

"There's nothing I can do right now, Dom. But I'll figure something out, I promise."

I checked my watch and discovered it was only a little after seven. The daylight and sunshine certainly helped lift my spirits, but when I gazed out to where the highway had once gone, I knew we needed to prepare for a long day of waiting.

Would the highway department be out or would they even bother with this mountain road? They hadn't closed it, so surely there would be people checking to see if anyone had gotten caught in the storm.

How could I have grown up in Colorado and not known the answers?

Easy. I'd never gone anyplace by myself. At least not beyond Bennington.

Pathetic.

Stick with the logical. Concentrate on the best possible outcome, that's what Zach always said. My brother, the optimistic, silly, lovable guy that always had a smile on his face.

Even when he was planning his own death.

I shook myself, refusing to allow any thoughts that could get me down.

So why did I think of Jonathan?

Hope that he might have contacted the authorities? Ridiculous. He not only wouldn't care, he'd probably rejoice. It would give him the opportunity to enact his plan to harm my family.

Mother had said not to worry about that. Now she'd been warned, she'd make sure Jonathan's threat never came to fruition. She, Daddy, and Granny Ed would all be safe. And if I didn't turn up, it was more likely Jonathan would be in trouble than the other way around.

The thought sent a little thrill through me.

"Sorry, Lord."

Bottom line, my family would make sure the authorities knew I was missing. Then there was Eric. Though I couldn't be sure if he got my message since it had beeped and disconnected before I'd finished speaking.

There had to be others who'd tried to cross the mountain last night. They'd be trapped, too. It was only a matter of time.

When I removed my scarf, my hair reacted crazily to the static. Domino barked at the sight, making me giggle.

My stomach growled loudly, a reminder that neither of us had eaten since sometime yesterday. A little snack was in order.

Domino munched happily on the small amount of food I gave her. Since most of the bottles of water were frozen solid, we had to share the little that wasn't. Not the best thing when eating a rather dry granola bar but better than nothing.

When we were finished, it was time to climb back over the console and attempt to open the driver's side door. I needed to go to the bathroom and figured Domino would need to as well.

"What do you think, girl? Let's just hope we don't freeze our tushies."

The seat was cold and hard and had a good deal of snow on it from the slit I'd left in the window last night.

The door panel had frosted over, giving me a warning that the next step wasn't going to be an easy one.

I pushed on the door, and though it sounded like it opened, nothing happened. It would take more than a shove from my shoulder to get outside. When I tried the handle again and felt no resistance, I knew what I had to do.

The console lid crunched when I settled my full weight on it. No reason to worry about that now. There were more pressing concerns.

I kicked at the door with all my might. Once, twice, three times. Snow piled in through the small opening, far more than I'd expected. I kicked again and again until the space was large enough for me to get outside.

Close to two feet of snow filled the area I'd kept relatively clear the night before. It formed a hard-packed wall around the car which had probably helped insulate us a bit. Once again, it took a lot of encouragement to get Domino to come out. Neither of us wasted time returning to the vehicle. It might be cold in the car, but it was definitely colder outside.

There was a struggle trying to reclose the door, but I knew it was a necessity. Since I couldn't shut the window, leaving the door open wasn't a viable option. Once it finally closed, I stuffed clothing from my suitcase into the small opening above the window. Hoping for a little warmth, I lit the candle, once again thanking my grandmother for insisting on the extras in the emergency kit.

"Maybe we should try to sleep some more, Dom." I tucked her blanket around her, set the tin can with its precious candle on the floor of the driver's side, and wrapped up in my blankets. Easing the seat back, I closed my eyes.

~~~

It was nearly nine when I returned to consciousness. The sun had begun to melt the ice on the windows and there was a little more warmth to the interior of the car. I tried to stretch, but with the cold and inactivity, my entire body felt stiff and sore.

It didn't take long to become stir crazy. Though I had to face the consequences of my actions, I would do it on my own terms. I couldn't just wait around for someone to save me. This was one battle I wouldn't give up without a fight. I needed a plan of action, some organization, before leaving the car. I wouldn't embark on this adventure without being fully prepared.

Adventure? That was a strange choice of word for my situation. True, I'd often prayed for something, for someone, to come save me from the life I led with Jonathan. I'd tried to be a good wife, staying in an impossible, abusive marriage because I didn't know what else to do. I'd pledged before God...

I'd twisted my faith in much the same way Jonathan had twisted our lives, tying everything into so many knots that it was soon unrecognizable. So, yes, I'd prayed for him to change, for our lives to be what they should. But God had given man free choice, which meant Jonathan could choose to remain the bent and cruel man he'd become.

And I had the right not to remain under his abusive thumb.

But running off into the night in pursuit of... What? The boy I'd once loved, the man I no longer knew? Not the right choice. And definitely not a smart one. I was
~~~

partway down a mountain road, overlooking a snow encrusted valley, miles from anywhere, with no idea whether I might be rescued or left to freeze. An adventure? Hardly. But maybe, just maybe, God would grant me the stamina I needed to get through the ordeal alive.

Now was the time to listen to that still, small voice. I bowed my head and prayed.

Chapter 31

I became a contortionist extraordinaire in the next hour, taking off my clothes and struggling into the different pieces Granny Ed had insured I had. God bless that dear, sweet woman for her intelligence and insight. And thank God for helping me get everything on without freezing in the long, drawn-out process.

Pantyhose, long johns, and the over-sized, flannel-lined jeans on my lower half, the top of the long johns followed by my sweatshirt, then one of the two wool sweaters from All Weather Gear made up my ensemble. It was a miracle I could still move around! Since I was sweating from all the activity, and couldn't face donning the parka now, I dug through my purse for necessities: my driver's license, a small bottle of Tylenol, my brush, and Mother's cell phone. Maybe if I got down the mountain a little, I'd be able to get service. I spotted a couple of safety pins at the bottom of the bag and knew immediately how to use them.

I took everything out of the basket, put the remaining sweater inside, then looked over at Domino. Because she was so small, the picnic hamper was the best way to carry her. Which meant I needed to reduce my stock so she'd have enough room inside.

When I grabbed her little blanket from the backseat and placed it inside the basket, Domino eyed me suspiciously. I added her bag of food, one roll of toilet paper, another emergency candle, matches, lighter, and light sticks. I stuffed the remaining five granola bars into my coat pockets, along with my license, the cell phone, the Tylenol, the doggie treats, one of the flashlights with extra batteries, and one bottle of water. Would it even be possible to move by the time I got into that parka? With the additional clothing I wore, and the weight of the items I'd placed into the pockets, I wasn't sure. And if I could move, the question remained whether or not I'd be able to carry the basket with Domino and the supplies.

"The rope!" I was surprised when Domino didn't give an answering bark. She still watched me warily, probably wondering if I'd lost my mind. Weird, but I actually felt like I'd *found* it.

I grabbed the pocketknife from where it still lay in the nearly empty box, and pulling the parka with me, kicked the door so hard, I tumbled outside. After tugging on the parka, I flipped the lever for the trunk. As I made my way to the back of the car, I prayed the trunk would open and my plan would work.

The first part of the prayer was answered—after pounding on the sides of the trunk several times. Then, with the rope in hand, I cut two six to seven-foot lengths which I then tied securely to the basket handles.

Next, I flipped the thermal blankets across my shoulders and snugged them around me with the aid of the safety pins.

I picked up an offended-looking Domino and placed her inside the basket.

"Don't worry, Dom, old buddy. It'll be like a sled ride. Like you know what that is. At any rate, it'll be a lot more comfortable than what I've got to look forward to." I closed the lid, slipped my scarf around my face, and was ready to go.

At the last minute, I reached back inside the car and dug in my purse until I found a pen and a scrap of paper. Wrenching off a glove, I scribbled a note with the direction I planned to go and then signed my name. Finished, I replaced the glove, but before shutting the car door, retrieved my sunglasses from the glove compartment. It was then I spotted the small New Testament—another gift from Granny Ed a long time ago. I tucked the Bible into an inside pocket of the parka, set my sunglasses in place, then headed down the hill. South, toward Allentown.

I'd no idea how far I was from my destination, but I refused to be daunted. There was no guarantee anyone would be searching for me, so remaining in the car seemed just as risky as trying to walk out of here—at least in my opinion. The feeling that my survival depended on helping myself was so overwhelming, it had to be the right thing to do.

"Here we go, old friend." I put the rope around my mid-section, tied the ends together, and started walking.

I'd never encountered such difficulty in all my life! Between the depth of the snow, the layers of clothing, and the weight of the picnic basket, every step was a struggle. Though I walked daily and exercised, I wasn't accustomed to such strenuous activity. It didn't take long for my heart to start pounding so hard I thought it would burst from my chest. And the bitterness of the air, in spite of the sun, made it hard to breath. But I kept on moving.

Every step was a test and a surprise. Sometimes the crackle and crunch of the snow sent me down nearly thigh high, other times the snowpack was so hard, I didn't fall through, just skated over the icy surface. For the most part, the basket seemed to skim across the top of the snow, making a minimal impression despite all the things inside. I, on the other hand, made it look as though Big Foot had trod through the area. It was a terrific path for a rescuer to follow.

It soon became apparent that using the car to gauge how far I'd gone was a mistake. Every time I looked back, I became disheartened by my lack of progress. Doubts began to set in, and to combat them, I sang Christmas songs, determined I would look only at what lay in front of me.

The scene before me was that of a vast wasteland of glistening whiteness and tall, majestic trees, their branches laden with snow. This stretched on as far as the eye could see and, I knew, even further. I had a long, arduous journey ahead of me that held no promises. No matter what happened, God would not desert me. Even if...

Defeatist thinking. Not today. Not today.

The sun shone down upon the snow with blinding intensity. My sunglasses helped, but it was still extraordinarily bright. Good thing I'd thought to grab them.

I reached the bottom of the first long hill a little after noon. Totally exhausted, and sweating from the exertion, I sat down on a log sticking out of the snow. My toes seemed warm enough with the thick wool socks and fur-lined boots, but the tips of my fingers were cold. As for my nose, I was fairly certain there were tiny icicles hanging from my nostrils. Not really, but it made me laugh.

Domino barked, reminding me of her presence.

"Just a moment, Dom." I said, clearing a spot near the log so she could get out. Finished, I released her from the basket and watched as she ran happily about.

I laughed as she rushed headlong from me to the furthest corner I'd cleared then back again. In those few moments we reveled in her freedom and temporarily forgot our plight.

Our moment was only that. It ended when we were startled by harsh, guttural growling which appeared to come from the edge of the woods. Squinting my eyes, and shielding them from the glare of the sun, I searched the area for the proprietor of the growl. There, standing barely visible, were several wild dogs or coyotes. I had no idea which and waiting to see if those animals wanted take a bite out of me just wasn't on my day's agenda.

I snatched Domino up just as she darted in the direction of those animals. I tucked her safely in the basket with a warning to stay put. I knew the old adage of not making any quick movements when faced by wild animals, but in this case, it would hardly apply. Right? I mean, slogging through snow an inch at a time could hardly be considered quick movement.

I continued my southerly journey as fast as my legs

and the snow would allow, opting to carry the basket rather than pull it behind. Though I figured Domino would adhere to my warning, I didn't want to chance it.

We were being stalked, the hairs on the back of my neck proved it, even if I couldn't actually see the animals. Being watched from the shadowy outline of the forest was disconcerting to say the least—terrifying, if I wanted to be more honest with myself. They were sly and treacherous, and far more equipped to move about in the snow than I was. But I couldn't, make that *wouldn't,* allow myself to think about it. Instead, I found myself lost in thoughts of the past, with memories I'd tried hard to erase. I knew why they were now crowding my brain and demanding attention. Dr. Harris had loosed something inside me, opened the flood gates that I'd determined would remain closed.

But there was something about this snow that reminded me of my brother. Zach had always loved winter. He and Tommy Lofgren had yearly sled competitions when we were kids. Mother even donated a trophy with a sledding figure on it that they would trade back and forth. Claire and I loved to watch the bigger kids on their sleds, flying down hills our parents had warned were not for us. Still, we'd trudge along after Zach and Tommy to stand on the sidelines while they, and friends like Eric, joined in the downhill races.

Each year, more and more kids would be drawn to the sledding hills, and every year parents throughout the community held their breath and hoped we'd all stay safe. Sure, there were a lot of wipeouts that resulted in some impressive black and blue marks and bruised egos, but that had been it. Until the year I was ten and Zach was thirteen.

He'd learned how to make his runners go even faster down the slopes by using a combination of steel wool and candle wax and was soon breaking speed records. He'd zoom past everyone, turning their heads and making them ooh and ahh at his sled and his ability. But Zach never let any of it go to his head. He took the accolades humbly, would wink at Claire and me, then move on to conquer yet another hill. One day, after hours on the slopes, he and Tommy had decided to take a break and just watch for a while. They tugged Claire and me over to the side for some of the hot chocolate Tommy's mother had sent along, leaving our sleds on the side of the hill as we always did. No one expected seven-year-old Davy Brown to swipe Zach's sled. What happened next was even more impossible to believe.

Zach had looked up when everyone on the hill yelled out a warning. I still remembered how his rosy cheeks had blanched, how he'd tossed the cup of chocolate into the snow and run to the edge of the hill. By then it was already too late to stop the runaway sled and the little boy who held so tightly onto it, screaming as it careened down that hill.

Although every kid in the area had run to the bottom, Zach got there first. The haunted look in his eyes when he turned to the rest of us said the news wasn't good. While Tommy and Claire went to get help, I sat in the snow with my brother, holding his hand and trying not to look at the broken body of the little boy that just peeked out from the thicket of bushes. It had taken a long time for the emergency personnel to get there, and I know for every second that passed, Zach felt worse and worse. By the time they'd carried Davy from the scene, Zach had been forever changed.

When we got home that evening, Zach hung up his sled in the garage, and there it remained to this day. No one blamed him for the accident—no one, that is, except Zach himself. He took the responsibility for Davy's death on his narrow shoulders, carrying it there for the rest of his life.

I'd been affected as well, as much by Davy's accidental death as by the way Zach responded to it. I'd watched as depression shrouded him within its cloak of darkness, watched as he struggled more and more to go on.

Two people died on the hill that day, Davy Brown went instantly; it took six years before it claimed its second victim.

I was brought back to the present abruptly when I tripped and fell into a snowbank. The snow stung my face and eyes, reminding me of my precarious situation. I frantically brushed the snow from my face and shoved my sunglasses back on in time to see Domino and the other contents of the basket spread out before me. I retrieved the objects as fast as possible before they had the chance to sink out of sight, then called to Domino. She slid across the encrusted snowbank, her tiny body trembling. I held her close, trying to calm her. When she'd stopped shaking, I tucked her back inside the basket and closed the lid on her sad little face.

After making one last check to ensure I'd picked up everything, I stood, prepared to continue forward. Pain shot up my right leg bringing tears to my already abused eyes.

"How can I do this with a sprained ankle?" I shouted, my voice echoing through the desolate valley to resound eerily back to me.

My ankle was beginning to stiffen, and I knew I had to push on before it was incapable of moving at all. If I thought the journey difficult before, I soon realized even more perseverance would be required.

"Help me, Father!"

Fear pushed me, but so did faith.

I hated having to walk parallel with the woods and the dark and frightening secrets they held. Until we were free of them, I would remain ultra-vigilant.

And would try to ignore the low growl coming from inside the basket.

Chapter 32

The languid sun peeked between two distant mountains lending amber, mauve, and pink to the darkening blue sky. The snow took on a sparkling star quality which added to the beauty of early evening.

Beautiful and deadly.

The strenuous activity, multi-layered clothing, and warmth of the mid-afternoon sun had kept the cold from penetrating my body. But when the temperature started to drop and night approached, it was a different story. And as the cold set in, I knew stopping meant certain death.

Was it a trick of the waning light, a mirage conjured up by an exhausted brain?

As I drew nearer, there was no doubt it was real. Nestled near the edge of the woods in the valley below sat a building of some kind.

Throughout the day I'd considered this journey an alternative to sitting in the car and awaiting an uncertain future. Though I'd hoped and prayed this headlong trek would be a solution to our problem, I had to admit being filled with doubts. But now, staring at the shadowy image before me, I knew I'd made the correct decision.

The boost of confidence was short-lived.

Believing I could remain cautious and still increase my speed from the painstaking plodding to something a bit faster, I rushed down the final hill. I *needed* to reach that building before it was completely dark.

I tumbled partway down the hillside, rolling in an ungraceful heap with the basket and belongings scattering about me. Once again, I was set the task of wandering about and gathering what I'd brought with me before it sank out of sight. Placing the items in the basket, I was surprised and pleased to find it was still in such good condition.

Domino waddled to me, wagging her tail when I lifted her from the snow.

"Not long now." I promised, tucking her back inside the basket. I closed the lid, wondering what she thought of this strange situation. In spite of being dumped from her hiding place twice, she appeared to be holding up pretty well.

Time to focus on the building in front of me.

And be a lot more careful as we continued forward.

Even with the plunge down the hill, it still took a good forty minutes before we reached it. For the first time in hours, I checked my watch. It was a little before six, and the light was fading fast. But even in the twilight, the building, which turned out to be an old log cabin, gave the appearance of solidity. It didn't matter if the mortar between some of the logs was nearly gone, nor would it matter if the wind pierced the cabin through those ancient cracks. It had a roof and four walls and would be a haven for the night to come.

I peered through the open doorway and was greeted with darkness. Before crossing the threshold, I paused long enough to pull the flashlight from my coat pocket and turn it on.

I released a slow, uneven breath as the light touched the various objects left in the one-room cabin. In the far corner lay a mattress upon a makeshift bed frame. The opposite corner had a large table, which looked relatively sound, and a couple of chairs in questionable condition. One of the chairs seemed to teeter on its three legs, unsure whether it should continue to stand or collapse on the filthy floor. A massive rocking chair sat to the left of the door, and the moldering blanket that covered it made me shiver in apprehension. On the west wall hung an iron skillet, and below that, a large kettle. Opposite these, was what appeared to be a built-in hutch.

I'd often heard tales of how prospectors and miners would desert their homes when their claims "pinched out," leaving the places almost entirely intact. I'd even been told a story once about a group of hikers who found a cabin complete with all the comforts of home. They'd stayed there weathering an oncoming storm and later returned to claim the place as their own. My cabin might not prove as providing, but it was my port in this storm.

I released Domino into our sanctuary and was instantly met with yelps of joy and approval. Though she ran into the darkness uninhibited, I followed with a bit more caution.

"This must have been built in the early nineteen hundreds." I walked through the piles of debris littering the floor and over to what had once been a beautiful stone fireplace.

"Why, it even has a mantel!" I ran my hand across it, revealing a bit of polished wood underneath all the scratches and filth. The cabin had once been well-cared-for.

A fireplace, Jessie.

The voice in my head made me take another look at my surroundings, at the trash on the floor, the pieces of a broken chair, and other items—all of which would be food for a fire.

"It's the answer to our prayers, Dom! I *know* this stuff will burn!"

I wanted to get a fire going immediately, not only for the warmth, but also for the light it would provide. Yes, I had another emergency candle and the light sticks, as well as the flashlight, but why use those if there was an alternative?

While hastening to separate the burnable items from the mess on the floor, I noticed snow packed in various places throughout the perimeter of the cabin. Once the fire was going, none of that would matter.

I carried everything that was usable over to the fireplace so it would be close at hand. When I discovered a small cache of wood beneath some old newspapers, I couldn't believe my good fortune.

The items were arranged with care, wood and paper intermixed in the hope they would catch the flame and burn long and sure. I closed my eyes, praised the Lord for providing us with shelter, added a wish that the flue was open and ready to go, then pulled the all-purpose lighter from the basket. My hand shook slightly as I ignited the paper and a few pieces of kindling in the grate.

I let out a sigh of relief as the smoke curled upwards and sent another thank you heavenward as warmth from the fire slowly began to thaw out a day's worth of cold.

Satisfied with the fire's progress, I decided to investigate my new home a little further. I went over to the bed and tugged gingerly on the mattress. When I pulled the thing off the frame and onto the floor, the mice, or rats, that had been living in it came as well. Startled, they scurried across my booted feet. As shocked as I was, I couldn't help giggling when Domino rounded them up and chased them out the door.

Odd, but until that moment, I hadn't even thought to see if there *was* a door. But there it was, still clinging to its hinges. I laughed at myself and went over to shut it, surprised at how I could have forgotten such an important thing.

Before closing out the night, I glanced into the twilight across "my" valley. This was an exquisite setting, and I could see why the owner had chosen to build here. But my tranquility was shattered by the sounds coming from the direction of the hill where I'd been just a short while ago. The animals I'd sighted earlier in the day were coming toward me, and from the looks of it, they'd be here soon.

I slammed the door and fastened it with the rusted deadbolt which was still in place. Windows! There were two, located on opposite sides of the cabin. I went directly to the north window. The dogs would reach it first.

If I'd had time, I would have cried for joy when I discovered its shutters not only in place, but also that they could be securely latched across the empty panes. As I ran to the other side of the cabin, my ankle reminded me of the afternoon's folly. Biting my lip against the stab of pain, I struggled to the other window.

The howling of the dogs as they neared the cabin sent a shiver of fear up my spine, spurring me on and pushing me past the pain.

Concentrating on the noise from outside, I prepared to latch the shutters on the south window only to find I wasn't as lucky this time. Although the shutters were still in place, they were not nearly as sturdy. I latched them as best I could, then stood back to watch and wait.

The cacophony of sound terrified me, but I hadn't been brought this far just to give up. I wasn't the only one affected by the howling; Domino sniffed the air, and her fur bristled. She paced the cabin, her little chest rumbling with her own deep growl. As the sound drew nearer, she paused to stare at me, wagged her tail, then placed herself directly in front of me. And so we waited.

I was shocked by the force of the attack when it came, the incessant pounding at the door and windows. The animals were trying their best to reach us, and I prayed for the continued strength of those bolts and hinges.

Panic ran through me, and I froze in terror. How could I protect us?

"No! I'm not going to die like this!"

With a determination I'd never felt before, I

grabbed a heavy board from among the debris and stationed myself at the south window. I was prepared to battle for our lives, and though my hands shook uncertainly as the first animal pushed its way through the shutters, I only hesitated a second before smashing my weapon across his head. I'd no sooner knocked one down than another forced his way in. Each time they were greeted with a blow from my weapon.

Gathering more courage, I slammed the shutters as another dog hurled himself forward. As I latched them, I heard the pained cries from the animals I'd injured. It was a pitiful sound that wrenched at my soul, but I refused to allow it to weaken me.

It wouldn't take long for them to regroup, which meant I needed to think of something fast. I quickly retrieved the iron skillet off the wall. With new-found strength, I drove the large spikes that held the shutters back into place. Having secured them the best I could at this time, I stood with my back against them, using my body as an additional barrier to thwart the animals' attempts to enter our refuge.

The strength and power the animals exhibited was unbelievable. Each time they flung themselves against the window, it was all I could do to remain at my post. I prayed they would give up and go away before my back gave out. I didn't relish the idea of standing guard with my board and bashing in their heads but was prepared to do so if it proved necessary.

By now, Domino was running insanely about the cabin, barking wildly. I had no words to comfort her and wasn't going to waste my energy trying. She continued her surveillance, acting far more courageous than I knew she was.

An hour passed and still they persisted, beating themselves against the cabin walls. Their determination to reach us was great, but mine would be greater.

Gradually, the assault decreased its intensity, and sometime after eight, it was over. My back ached from the beating it had taken, and my legs grew weaker by the second. I looked at the mattress with longing, wishing I could pull it close to the fire and collapse upon it. Allowing sleep to take possession of my mind and body would be a pleasant relief, but I couldn't grant myself that luxury yet. I'd no idea if my tormentors would return, but in the event they did, I knew preparing now was a necessity.

After feeding my fire, I attempted to repair the shutters on the south window. Using the iron skillet once again, I hammered the spikes until they were securely in the walls. I added to the security by fitting a rung from the broken chair into the latch lock. Finished, I tested my handiwork, disappointed it wasn't as strong as I'd hoped. It might not stand up to another attack like the one we'd just weathered, but it would offer more protection than before.

I checked the door and the other window, thankful to find they'd withstood the assault without any visible signs of stress. By the time I was finished, exhaustion threatened to overtake me. I pulled the mattress over to the fireplace, checked to make certain there were no more creatures living in or around it, then collapsed in a heap.

I stared into the depths of the fire, longing for the comfort and security of my own home.

But Jonathan would be there, and that wasn't acceptable. Not anymore.

Domino settled in next to me, her dark eyes reflecting her love and devotion. I patted her, drawing her close.

The necessity to keep the fire going caused me to sleep fitfully. I'd awaken long enough to feed the flames, then lapse back into a semi-conscious state where nothing appeared as it should. I think the wild dogs came back, thought I heard them, but couldn't be sure.

Sometime during the night, I awoke dizzy and disoriented. My eyes burned and nausea crept through me. I was acutely aware of pain in my throat, ears, back, and ankle. A part of me wanted to find the bottle of Tylenol in hopes of relief, but it lost out to the other part that demanded I rest.

Before passing out once again, a terrifying thought occurred to me.

"Maybe I'm dying."

ALICE K. ARENZ

214

Chapter 33

Zach sat on the edge of my bed, his head in his hands.

"Nobody ever blamed you," I told him, pulling on his sleeve, trying to get him to look at me. "It wasn't your fault. Davy made a choice to swipe your sled, Zach. You didn't force it on him. If he'd wanted a ride, all he had to do was ask. I know you'd have taken him down the hill like you did the rest of us."

He rubbed his face, removed his hands, and sat staring in front of him. I studied his profile, from the smooth high forehead to his angular jaw line. I'd always considered my brother good-looking, Claire insisted he was drop-dead gorgeous. Right now, the depression that had sent him spiraling into the depths of hell, and his haunted expression, reflected neither.

"You don't understand, Jess. No one can." He pushed off the bed and went to stand before the only window in my room. After punching at the air in front of him, he shoved his hands into the pockets of his windbreaker.

Over his shoulder I could see the first streaks of burnished gold as the sun began to rise. I had about fifteen minutes before the alarm went off, and I had to get ready for school. I'd rather stay home and keep Zach company, but Mr. Cord, my English teacher, wouldn't like it if I missed the mid-term.

I switched off the alarm then climbed from bed.

"I told him no." Zach said quietly.

"Who?"

"Davy." He turned around, dark against the brightening sky behind him. "I was too busy showing off, acting like I was king of the hill. When he started bugging me about a ride, I told him to get lost."

I shook my head, trying to wrap my sleepy brain around what he was telling me.

"He asked you to give him a ride? You never said anything about that before."

"Never told anyone, really, till recently."

I could tell by the sound of his voice that someone besides me knew this secret. "Who else knows?"

"Pastor Nickerson."

"What did he say?" I swallowed hard, knowing the answer would never satisfy my brother.

Zach shrugged his shoulders then sauntered over to the door. "Doesn't matter."

"It's still not your fault, Zach. You've got to believe that."

He stopped at the door and gazed over at me. "You know why I refused to give the kid a ride? He was coughing and sneezing all over the place, and snot was running from his nose. It was disgusting." He continued to watch me, waiting for a response. I didn't have one.

"That's why he's dead, Jess. Because I didn't want his germs all over my precious sled." Zach grabbed hold of the door and yanked it open. He stopped on his way out, put his head against the jamb and whispered, "And for that, I got his blood."

~~~

The memory followed me up from sleep, an accusation that I hadn't done enough to keep my brother alive.

I awoke with a start, acutely aware of the tremendous cold all around me. It took several seconds before I realized the fire had gone out. And from the looks of it, had been out for quite some time.

Both my back and ankle were stiff from my previous day's activities, and because of the cold, the rest of my body suffered as well. My laborious movements made it difficult to maneuver with any great speed, so it seemed to take forever to fill the fireplace with most of what was left in my pile of "burnables." My fingers were cramped with cold and ached when I pressed and held the lighter to ignite the scraps of paper. By the time the fire blazed, I was exhausted. I sat on the thin, filthy mattress and lost myself in the dancing flames. Domino crawled over to join me, and we huddled together, glad for one another's company.

After a while, I gazed around the room, taking stock of my surroundings with the aid of sunlight peeking in through cracks in the shutters and walls. Skiffs of snow drifted across the floor towards us only to melt as they neared the flames. As the chill dispersed from my body in much the same fashion, I decided it
~~~

was time to explore the cabin and the outside area surrounding it. At the very least, I needed to find downed branches to dry out for eventual use in the fireplace.

I lumbered to my feet, stretched, then began my investigation.

The table wasn't as sturdy as it looked last evening with only the beam of the flashlight shining upon it. The filtered sunlight revealed that both the tabletop and legs were suffering from rot. But even through these signs of decay, I could tell it had once been beautiful. I ran my hand across the cool oak and thought what a shame it was that it had been left here to be defaced by the weather and vandals who had carved their initials and nasty messages into it. It was obvious the piece had been built by someone with an eye for detail and considerable talent.

At the far end of the table, I discovered two drawers in the bottom side. After trying to open them several times, one suddenly freed itself and sent me, and its contents, flying backward. I gazed in wonder at the tarnished silverware and other cooking utensils strewn about the floor. Since I still held the drawer, it was an easy task to clean up the mess. I replaced the drawer, then pulled on the other one until it began to dislodge. This time, however, I was more careful, and when the drawer came free, was prepared.

Old newspapers lined this drawer. I lifted them, searching for other hidden treasures, but found nothing.

I went on to examine the kettle and the iron skillet I'd used as a hammer the night before. The bottoms of both were rusted, but not badly, which surprised me. The skillet was maybe twelve inches and resembled the ones my grandmother referred to as spiders. The kettle was the largest I'd ever seen and was very heavy. It was about a foot and a half deep, at least as wide, and was equipped with heavy-duty handles on either side. If I couldn't figure out something else to use, it would be the perfect chamber pot.

Domino must have been thinking along the same lines. She stood at the door and barked, ran to me, then raced back to the door. I didn't hear any sounds coming from outside but wasn't about to just open the door and let her out without checking first. Once I'd made certain it was safe, I let her pass. She sniffed the air, appeared to gauge the depth of the snow, then jumped out onto the sketchy little porch. It didn't take long for either of us to get back inside.

Returning to my investigation, I moved to the built-in hutch.

The windows had been broken from the doors a long time ago, but tiny pieces of what appeared to be frosted glass still clung to the frame. I tugged at one of these till it rested in my hand and fingered it thoughtfully. The miner who had lived in this cabin had obviously been married; there was no other explanation for the nice table and frivolous little hutch. The stories I'd heard repeatedly stated how lightly those people traveled, as they were never certain of their stay in any one place. The hutch spoke of a woman's touch, as did the polished wood on the mantel and table.

The shelves of the hutch were breaking up from decay and held no treasures except for what resembled a master key. Unbelievably, it fit and unlocked the bottom two doors of the hutch. These shelves contained broken china, mismatched stoneware, and several pieces of tin ware: cups, dishes, and what appeared to be some prospector's tools. Even more amazing were the tins of beans! Several rusted cans sat untouched in the same spot they'd been for years—or so the dirt on them appeared.

"Yum." I laughed and received a bark of agreement from Domino.

The bottom shelves had been lined in the same fashion as the drawers of the table, the newspapers now yellowed with age and crumbling to the touch. As with the ones in the drawers, they were dated from just before the turn of the century and boasted of gold and silver strikes, lawless boom towns, and loose women.

"The good old days." I laughed again, happy to still possess a sense of humor.

Tucked behind the beans and tin ware was a good-sized porcelain bowl, a little chipped around the top, but perfect for use as an indoor toilet!

All the comforts of home, or almost. I could use a little something to eat.

After pouring a small amount of Domino's food onto the cleanest plate I could find, I dug out one of the five remaining granola bars and what was left of my bottle of water. Moving to the rocking chair, I gingerly lifted the mildewed blanket and tossed it to the floor. I tested the chair for strength before sitting down. Satisfied it would hold my weight, I tugged the chair closer to the fireplace. I munched on half the granola bar, determined to save the rest for later. When Domino finished her meal, she joined me. We sat there rocking, enjoying the fire and this temporary reprieve.

With all the stuff left in the cabin, it made me wonder if the owner had thought about returning one day. When he hadn't, the place had been left to decay in the wilderness, becoming the home of the mice I'd seen last night, and other creatures who stumbled upon it. Human occupation from time to time was apparent by the debris and small pile of kindling I'd found. The fact no one had destroyed the cabin and its possessions was amazing.

Time passed and the room dimmed. The wind whistled through the cracks, blowing in little wisps of snow that would dance about then fall gracefully to the floor. I was thankful for the comforting warmth of the fire filling the small cabin, especially now it was snowing again.

It was nearing four o'clock. My second day was almost over. In spite odds and ends of discomfort, I was fine. But before night closed in, I figured an exploration of the immediate area outside the cabin was in order. Though the fire still blazed, the pile of "burnables" had diminished. It was necessary to replenish my wood supply.

I lifted my sleeping dog from my lap, and as I laid her upon the mattress, she stirred, opened her eyes, stretched, yawned, then closed her eyes once again. I stroked her back gently, thankful for her companionship.

After removing the safety pins from the thermal blankets that still hung about my shoulders, I placed them on the table, then retrieved my pocketknife and the large knife I'd found in the drawer. I wrapped the scarf around my head and braced myself to face the cold as I stepped out into the snow.

Once again, I admired the beauty of the valley and the velvety whiteness around me. But the more it snowed, the more those lovely crystals hindered my chances of rescue.

I couldn't blame my situation on the weather. It had been foolish to disregard the advisory, to turn off the radio and run headlong into the coming storm.

I'd told my mother I wanted to escape, had used the same terminology when the tow company returned my car.

Be careful what you wish for.

Forcing the disturbing thoughts from my mind, I concentrated on the more important concern in front of me: survival.

Wanting to stay in close proximity to the cabin, I studied the area carefully before venturing beyond the rickety porch. I glanced in the direction of the hill where the dogs had come the night before, checked and rechecked the crest to make certain they were nowhere in sight, then stood with my eyes closed and listened. When all I could hear was the soughing of the trees bent and laden with their burdens of snow, my confidence soared and I moved cautiously from my shelter and over to the small stand of trees on the cabin's south side.

Wading through snow that had deepened overnight, I wondered how to get the branches I'd need. I was far too short and, dressed as I was, too cumbersome to climb the trees even if I could reach the lower limbs.

My concerns were quickly laid to rest. The weight of the snow and velocity of the winds had broken several of the smaller branches, scattering them about on the snow. I picked up as many as I could carry and trudged back to the cabin. After placing them inside the door, I headed back for more.

It was becoming a habit with me, and not a good one. For the third time in the last two days, I tripped, landing headfirst into a snowbank. Furious, I started to pull myself upright when I noticed something lying next to me in the drift. It took only a moment to recognize it as one of the wild dogs. Transfixed in terror, I remained motionless, fearing to even blink, afraid the slightest movement might bring on an attack. My heart thundered in my chest, pounding against my ribs painfully as it restricted my breathing. Snow melted inside my boots and gloves, and I fought to repress a shiver as icy tentacles radiated throughout my body.

It took awhile to work up the courage to investigate the animal, and when I realized he was dead, I felt like celebrating.

"You must have been one of my victims last night." My voice broke the silence of the late afternoon and echoed through the small valley.

I brushed the snow from the dog and noticed the top of his head had nearly been crushed. The sight churned my stomach, and I turned away to keep from vomiting. When my stomach calmed, I covered the animal with piles of snow while asking for forgiveness. Perhaps that was naive, but it was my way of coming to terms with taking a life.

Even though I'd been protecting Domino and myself.

Chapter 34

Domino barked and wagged her tail when I stepped through the doorway. She started toward me but stopped in her tracks, not certain she should approach me with all the branches in my arms. I called out to reassure her, dropped what I carried onto the floor, then gave her a quick pat before going out for another load.

Though my hands were cold and ached, I only stopped to warm myself a couple of minutes. I wanted to collect more of the downed branches before it got any darker.

This time, I encouraged Domino to come with me. She was hesitant at first, careful to stay near the cabin steps. But the more I traveled back and forth from the tree line, the more adventurous she became. Soon, she was using the path I'd made as a run, gleefully going from point to point, barking and nipping at the snowflakes.

I filled an entire side of the cabin with the limbs, knowing they'd have to dry out before they could be used in the fireplace. I figured the more I had, the better it would be. Once I got the last load inside, I grabbed the skillet and kettle to fill with snow. But first I needed to find a way to clean them—or, at least, give it a try.

It had stopped snowing, but the sky retained most of the clouds and still looked threatening. I idly wondered if anyone had missed me yet, when, suddenly, I knew one person who would have: Granny Ed. When I hadn't gone to her house yesterday, she would've called Jonathan to find out where I was. And if he didn't answer, she'd have gone to the police.

"She'll make sure they find me," I said with certainty. Granny Ed would camp out at the police station until she was satisfied something was being done!

Buoyed by the thought, I attacked the task at hand. I broke off several icicles lining the low roof, formed, I assumed, during the short-lived warmth of the day before. I put them to work on the interior of the skillet and kettle, scrubbing for ten to fifteen minutes before admitting it was hopeless. I filled them both with snow and carted them inside. As I closed the door, darkness descended over the valley, plunging it into an oppressive blackness that gave me the willies.

After filling the empty water bottle with snow, I put some into a tin cup and placed it near the fireplace to melt. Domino nipped at it, shook her little body, then sat back to watch me.

The one place I had yet to investigate was a shelf above the north window. I thought I could see something up there, but try as I might, couldn't reach whatever it was. I finally grabbed a small branch and ran it across the shelf. A bundle of old candles rained down on me.

Gazing at my new-found hoard, I decided to be decadent.

Retrieving several of the tin cups from the hutch, I melted the ends of four candles so they would adhere to the tin ware. By the time I'd finished and placed them at various points around the cabin, they'd transformed my humble abode into one of old-fashioned, homey comfort. The soft yellow glow met with Domino's approval. Especially when I opened a packet of her treats and poured the contents onto a plate.

She wriggled all over in anticipation, jumping onto the three-legged chair and tipping it so she nearly fell. Normally well-mannered, my little dog put her paws on the table, anxious for something to eat.

"Just a sec, girl." I said, putting the plate on the floor. "Tonight we eat by candlelight."

She jumped down and practically inhaled the treats in a matter of seconds.

When she was done eating, she went back to the cup near the fire and lapped up the water from the melted snow.

The branches seemed to insulate the cabin. So much so that I decided it was safe enough to remove a little of my excess clothing. I draped my scarf across the sturdiest of the chairs and put my gloves on the seat. It would give them a chance to dry before I'd need them again. I'd have liked to take off the parka, but a sudden gust of wind and skiffs of snow coming in through the cracks made the decision for me. I kept the coat on and sank into the rocker.

I ate the other half of my granola bar as the candles flickered and danced, sending shadows throughout the room. I watched their gentle sway, seeing a rhythm in the way they moved. It lulled my weary mind, giving me a sense of serenity. After a while, I went around and blew them out, knowing it would be wise to save them for tomorrow.

Glancing at my watch, I noticed it was close to midnight; time to settle down for sleep. Yet, as much as I desired sleep, I found myself lying awake and listening to the crackling fire and Domino's contented snoring. Once, I thought I heard an owl and some howling off in the distance. I started to get up, then sank back onto my pallet.

"Just don't come back." I said wearily.

Yawning, I closed my eyes, ready to dream. This was all a nightmare, none of it could really be happening, could it? I would awaken in the morning in my own bed to find I'd suffered some sort of delirium.

Didn't want that. Didn't want that.

As I drifted off to sleep, I knew the truth. And the one thing I didn't want was a home with Jonathan.

Reason floated beyond my reach, and sinking into the realms of sleep, I knew I was within the arms of an angel.

Chapter 35

I was in the middle of my English mid-term when Mrs. Wilson, the principal, came to pull me from class. Even without her somber expression, I knew something serious had happened.

Mrs. Wilson directed me to get my things, followed behind me as I did so, then stood at the front door until Pastor Nickerson arrived. The adults barely looked at one another as they conducted me out to the pastor's car. By the time Nickerson got behind the steering wheel, I was about to jump out of my skin.

"Has something happened to my parents?" I asked, saying a quick prayer that if one of them had been in an accident, it *wouldn't* be Daddy. I sent an apology heavenward, asking God to understand what was difficult for me to explain, or even admit. I held my breath and waited.

"Jessie," Peter Nickerson's voice cracked. He turned to me, a tear trickling down his right cheek.

"Please just tell me and get it over with."

"Zach's in the hospital, Jessie. He, he missed the bridge south of town, went into the river."

"That's not possible." I shook my head in denial.

"The car was partially submerged. By the time they got to him-"

"We were together this morning before school. He was working things out. *Talking to you.*"

"We don't know how long he was there before paramedics arrived. He wasn't breathing, but they managed to revive him-"

"No!" I didn't want to hear what he said, refused to believe it. "Just drive, don't talk. *Get me to the hospital*!"

He took me at my word, continuing the trip in silence. He hadn't come to a complete stop before I was out of the car and dashing in through the emergency entrance. People stared at me, someone even tried to stop me from running through the hallway. I threw off their hands, jerked away, and kept on going. I knew the way to the ICU by heart, could probably have gotten there with my eyes closed. All the other times had turned out all right. So would this one.

Mother stood in the waiting room, her face so white and still I thought Pastor Nickerson had been mistaken, that she was the accident victim and not my brother. She leaned against the doorway, one hand on the jamb, the other wrapped around a gold chain Zach had given her last Christmas. Even now, she retained that regal, standoffish aura that seemed to enshroud her the majority of the time. There wasn't anything about her that spoke of helplessness or need. These occasions always had her running through scenarios on how to downplay what had happened to the press. Heaven forbid anyone should find out a member of the mayor's family wasn't as perfect as Ellen Randolph insisted they appear.

I wanted to yell at her, make her see that all her pretense of perfection is what led us to this moment. Tell her that every time Zach tried to hurt himself had been a cry for help not a selfish, spoiled kid looking for a way to punish his parents. Deep down, Daddy knew the truth, even if he couldn't understand it. But Mother regarded it as a betrayal by her favorite child. Admitting Zach had a problem would be admitting she wasn't the model of domesticity she wanted everyone to believe she was.

I turned away before my anger made me say something I'd regret. As I neared the nurse's station, Granny Ed came out of a nearby room. Her sweet face looked shell-shocked.

"Jessie, honey, why don't you come with me?" She reached for my hand, but as much as I loved her and wanted the comfort she'd provide, I needed to see Zach.

She allowed me to go. As I passed her, she patted my shoulder.

"I'll be in the waiting room, sweetheart."

A nurse looked up when I entered the room. I remembered her from the time Zach OD'd last year. She'd always been attentive and encouraging with a ready smile and a joke. Now, she shook her head, then continued to disconnect her equipment.

"Mr. Randolph, sir?" Her voice was kind as she addressed my father. "Sir, you and your daughter can have a few more minutes before we need to-"

"Please go." Daddy didn't look up, just continued

to stare at the still form in the bed.

Could I be dreaming? That's how it felt, surreal yet intense. I moved forward, my eyes fastened on Zach's face. He was so pale, so very pale.

I don't remember those last steps, only know I could hear shouting and a sound that reminded me of a wounded animal. From Daddy's reaction, I knew it was coming from me, but it didn't connect.

Zach's hands and face were cold and clammy. No matter how many times I yelled his name and shook him, he didn't respond. How could they move him from the ICU when he was still so sick? It didn't make any sense.

The next thing I remembered was the church. I sat in a pew to the side of the sanctuary, a place always reserved for members of the family during a funeral. Though I didn't know how I'd gotten there, I knew why. But still I believed my brother *could not be inside that box*, that coffin. That was the first step toward breaking my heart.

And my spirit.

Chapter 36

To my surprise, I awakened the next morning rested and energized. Sunlight streamed into the cabin, bringing with it a touch of warmth.

The branches I'd brought in the afternoon before seemed to have dried out fairly well, so I stoked the fire with a few of them. Domino and I drank more of the snow water while we ate. There wasn't much left of the food I'd brought for her, though I still had a couple packets of treats. As for me, I couldn't settle for half the granola bar today. My stomach demanded the entire thing.

For the first time since the ordeal started, I removed my coat. As I draped the bright yellow parka on the rocker, I couldn't help giving it a grateful pat. Granny Ed had been right in choosing that particular coat—color and all.

It felt so good to be freed from the weight of the parka! I stretched and scratched all over, then went through a series of exercises until I was so weak I collapsed on the mattress, laughing. Domino jumped on top of me, and we wrestled about playfully.

After a while, I bundled back up so I could collect more branches. When I opened the door, I could scarcely believe my eyes. It snowed again during the night, obliterating all signs of footprints, or prints of any other kind. The glistening snow lay thickly on the tree branches, making them bow down as if in homage to its dazzling beauty. Dainty star flakes danced in the sunlight, revealing a special meaning to the crystallized world outside: in spite of the cabin seeming warmer, the temperature had actually dropped and frozen the downy flakes into an encrusted ensemble. This enabled Domino and I to walk upon the glaze, leaving very little sign of our passing. We treaded with care, fearful we'd find a soft patch we might sink into.

"It would swallow you up like quicksand, Dom. I'd never be able to save you." I hoped she understood the warning in my voice.

In spite of the crispness of the morning air, the sun felt warm upon my face, making it tolerable. We took our time gathering the branches for kindling, and I was glad for something to occupy my mind.

As we returned to the cabin with our final load, I noticed something moving about near the cabin. Spying it, Domino ran to the object. She barked wildly as she darted to, then away from it. She repeated the action several times before I reached her.

Drawing closer, I could see the small ball of grayish colored fur and recognized the "object" as a rabbit. It appeared to be having some sort of trouble with its hind legs—try as it might to extricate itself from whatever held it, it could not. And Domino's madness didn't help matters; the poor thing was terrified. My natural instinct urged me to help the animal. But these were not ordinary circumstances.

Instead of freeing the rabbit, I found myself squeezing the life from that small, helpless creature. It flopped pathetically about in my hands, then, with a great shudder, lay still.

I sat there in the snow, looking at what I'd done, shocked at having taken its life. Then, brushing tears from my eyes, I picked up my prey and returned to the cabin.

Chapter 37

I'd never had the experience of cleaning game, never cleaned a fish. The closest I'd come to such a thing was washing a turkey and removing the prepackaged giblets from inside it. But, as I'd already discovered, when pushed, a person could do a lot more than they thought they were capable of doing.

I tucked my conscience and disgust away in a tidy corner of my brain. There must be some imbedded instinct for survival that told me the necessary steps to follow. I didn't know, didn't want to know or even think about it. From the time I'd returned to the cabin, until the moment I first smelled the roasting meat, I'd been on a strange sort of auto-pilot.

While the meat sizzled in the fireplace, I decided to repair some of the cracks in the walls. The tattered blanket that had been on the rocking chair when I'd first arrived might be moldy and threadbare but would serve quite well as a filler for the large crack in the east wall.

But when I tried to stuff it into the crevice, I ran into a problem. Taking my flashlight, I shined it into the hole, reached a cautious hand inside, and pulled out a wad of newspapers. As I headed to the fireplace to toss them in, a necklace of love beads fell onto the floor. Picking them up, I noticed a note attached.

"To whomever finds this: Let it be known that God, and we, love you. Sunshine & Peace, 1967."

The message was simple, but it made me feel warm inside. I looked toward the shuttered south window and stepped into the swath of sunlight streaming in. As I did so, an incredible peace descended over me.

I put the necklace around my neck, letting it hang on the outside of my coat. Strange, but just by touching the beads, I didn't feel so lost and forgotten. This message from the past reached out to give me a reassurance of my future.

I finished "repairing" the crack in time to turn the meat. A heavenly aroma filled the air, causing my mouth to water. The way Domino paced back and forth in front of the fireplace, I knew she felt the same anticipation I did.

But no matter how hungry I was, the bitter reality of rationing the food supply was uppermost in my mind. I'd no idea how long we'd be here, so it was imperative to stay with tiny meals. No more eating an entire granola bar at one time. There were only three left. Those, and the rabbit, needed to last as long as possible.

We ate together that afternoon, relishing our little meal. Finished, the remainder of the meat was sandwiched between two plates, then encased in one of the old newspapers I'd found in the hutch. I placed it onto the shelf where I'd discovered the candles, knowing the cold air coming in behind it would keep the meat as well there as if inside a refrigerator.

I scrubbed our dishes in the snow and then collected more of the frosty stuff to melt. While Dom curled up before the fire to nap, I gathered the remaining newspapers and sat in the rocker to read them.

One of the papers, from a long defunct Bennington press, was dated June 1909. The others, from both Bennington and Allentown, had dates ranging from the 1920's to 1967. They were filled with happenings of days long past and forgotten, but they stimulated my mind and allowed me a momentary oblivion to the present.

Reading the papers reminded me of the small Bible I'd brought with me. I lit the emergency candle and the tapers I'd found the night before, then settled into the chair. This particular New Testament also included Psalms, so I decided on my favorite: Psalm 23. I read it over and over, the words, as always, comforting me. Still, the day seemed to go by slower than the previous ones. It led to idle thoughts, incongruous to the peace I'd felt reading the Psalm.

I wondered if Eric got any part of the message I'd tried to leave. Had he found someone else to help with backing vocals for his concerts? Had he thought about me at all? And what about my parents? Surely Granny Ed would've told them I'd gone missing.

But Mother knew I wanted to escape. She'd given me her cell phone. Even if my grandmother contacted the police, there was the possibility that Mother's information stopped them from looking into it.

Only Granny Ed would sound the alarm. Would that be enough?

Matt Harris might join his concern with hers. I'd made a point of letting him know I intended to see him for my appointment. When I hadn't shown up...

The cell phone! Why hadn't I thought of it till now?

Because I'm not used to having one, of course.

I searched through the hamper and my coat, unable to find it. Searched again and again, finally accepting I must have lost it during one of my tumbles in the snow. How could I have let that happen? Why hadn't I been more careful?

No signal.

Maybe. But I'd never know.

After feeding the fire and blowing out the candles, I huddled down next to Domino, more than a little disheartened.

"Please, Lord, please let us be found soon. I know I've never done much of anything for You, that I haven't lived my life the way You would've liked, but..."

But what? I'd tried bargaining with God in the past, begging for Him to take it back, to rewind time and let Zach live. If only I'd stayed home that morning instead of going to school, maybe Zach would still be alive. I might have found the right words to say to him, to Daddy... or to Mother.

I knew Zach was sick, knew it better than any of them... Knew it before he'd tried to commit suicide that first time.

He had a habit of coming to my room early in the morning when things were bothering him. Our special bond and trust in one another meant we could share anything without worrying it would be passed along. I couldn't count the times I'd find him sitting on the end of my bed, watching me sleep. Those were mostly happy times. But that changed the last two years of his life.

I'd awaken to find his dark eyes hooded, his face a study of bewilderment. That was a sign he'd spent another sleepless night, brooding over the past and what he should have done. He'd talk about the day Davy stole his sled and taken that fateful ride. Sometimes, he would openly blame himself. Mostly, though, he would talk in terms of what if, or the should haves we speak of when we wish there'd been some way to change the outcome of something. After the second time this happened, I'd known he would try to hurt himself. That's the reason his overdose hadn't been successful. But that last morning, I'd been so worried about my mid-term it hadn't connected. The moment he'd mentioned Davy Brown...

No excuse. *I should have known.*

Tears streamed down my face and I buried it into Domino's soft fur.

I'd been sixteen, worried about mid-terms—and the senior trip Eric was leaving on that weekend. A girl in his class had been sidling up to him for days, telling everyone she planned on stealing him away from me. So, when my brother awakened me that morning, I'd been so wrapped up in what was going on in my own life that I hadn't allowed the warning signs to register. Five hours later, Zach was dead.

"I'm sorry," I cried, turning my eyes heavenward. "I let him down, God. I know I did, and it was selfish. I can't ask him to forgive me, Father, but I can ask You, right? I, I don't want to carry this burden around any longer. I don't want to end up like Zach. Please, Father, I want to be a better person. *I want to live.*"

It sounded so typical, so ineffectual. I didn't know if I could be a better person when, or if, I got out of here. I knew I wouldn't be the same one who'd started this journey, but better?

I must have cried myself to sleep because the next thing I knew it was dark, the fire nearly out. I hastened to feed it before lighting the emergency candle. It wasn't as inviting as having the old candles lit throughout the cabin, but at least it dispelled the darkness.

Rather than eat an evening meal, I encouraged Domino to drink more water. It wasn't as satisfying, especially when I knew we had food. Domino turned her nose up at the water and began pacing the length of the cabin, growling deep within her chest. I called to her several times, but she ignored me and continued the strange behavior.

Shrugging her off, I grabbed the kettle and leaned out the door to collect more snow to melt. I was nearly finished when I heard the soft crunching of something moving stealthily across the ice encrusted bank opposite me. It was so quiet, I thought it must be a small animal out foraging for food. It wasn't until I stood up to close the door that I saw them.

Four of the wild dogs were within six feet of me, standing just inside the circle of light emitting from the cabin. My heart thundered, and as I slammed the door, the animals lunged forward.

"Dear God, not again!" My head felt light, but my

arms and legs were dead weights. Try as I might to move, I was unable to do so. I stood there, foolishly listening to the sound of those predators beating themselves against the cabin walls as I did nothing.

How could I freeze up now? I needed to pull myself together!

I tried moving again and was suddenly aware I'd fallen to the floor.

"Must have fainted." I mumbled. "Must have fainted." Only that could account for my inability to function.

My hands and feet tingled from the lack of blood, and my head seemed to have swollen to twice its size. Perhaps it was only my imagination, but I could have sworn I felt the hot breath of the dog outside the door as he sniffed around the cracks and crevices.

But the clicking sound of his claws on the frozen wood of the small porch wasn't my imagination.

With only the ancient door between us, a menacing growl had me struggling to my feet. I stomped around in an effort to restore my circulation as I scanned the cabin for a weapon. Where was the board I'd used before? I didn't know, and there wasn't time to look for it. I grabbed the kettle off the floor, dumped the snow, and waited.

Barking and growling came at us from every side. As the feverish pitch grew in intensity, Domino suddenly ceased her frenetic pacing and crept toward one of the larger cracks in the floor on the south side. Her nose twitched, and the hair on her back bristled. What had her so upset?

Kneeling, I looked down and saw eyes staring up at me from only a few inches away. I flew back with a scream just as a snout shoved its way in through the crack, teeth bared. I pounded the kettle into its face, heard a yelp, then moved away, keeping my eyes fixed on the floorboards.

The kettle had worked, but not as well as I'd hoped. Reaching behind me to the table, I searched for something, anything to use as a weapon.

My fist closed on the handle of the iron skillet, and I brought it forward with as much power as I could. The piercing cry of the animal as the skillet connected sent a satisfying thrill through me—until I noticed the splintering of the wood surrounding the crack. The yelps and cries of the animal as it withdrew, had me back on my knees, shoving branches into the crack.

Domino remained at my side, a menacing growl shaking her tiny body. When I couldn't stuff anything else into the area, I stumbled to the south window—the other weak point of the cabin. I'd no idea if the shutters would withhold another battering, and after the close encounter a moment before, wasn't about to take any chances. Still holding the skillet, I grabbed the three-legged chair and prepared myself for the battle ahead.

But it never came. Instead, a new sound slashed through the night and echoed throughout the valley. Could it be?

Domino shivered at my feet, her dark eyes peering up at me in fear as she melted against my legs.

The barking and growling of the dogs moved away from the cabin, becoming even more frenzied than before. Yelps and screams, the unmistakable sounds of a fight, whining and crying from the dogs that turned my insides to jelly. It sounded like a mountain lion was tearing those animals to shreds.

I put my hands over my ears trying to block out the terrible noises. As the racket slowly died down, a new fear came over me. I waited at the window an hour, clenching the skillet in my hands until my knuckles were white and my fingers stiff. Was I prepared to face a new and even more terrifying enemy?

I remained at my post until I could no longer stand. I stumbled over to the mattress and collapsed. Pulling the thermal blankets over my head, I sank into the depths of sleep with a prayer for deliverance on my lips.

ALICE K. ARENZ

Chapter 38

Eric had been there to comfort me, to help me pick up the pieces of my life. Between him and Claire, I'd had shoulders to cry and lean on when my parents had become distant and cold. They were there to witness the warmth and zest for life seep from my father until all that was left was a shell of his former self. Everyone said that time would heal the wounds left by Zach's suicide. But most people hadn't known the full extent of my brother's depression and the toll it had taken on my family. Claire and Eric knew, though, and they were among the few that didn't put salve on the sore and then expect it to magically be all better. They'd seen firsthand the devastation that rocked my family and tried to destroy us all. And no one knew this better than Zach's best bud, Tommy Lofgren.

I often found Tommy up in the rickety old tree fort the boys had made when they were kids. He'd try to hide the tears in his eyes when I came upon him like that, but he wasn't successful. Zach's loss hit Tommy about as hard as it hit the rest of us. They'd always planned on going away to college together and doing all the things guys did when they were out from under the watchful eyes of their parents. When he'd left for school the year before, Zach had assured Tommy he'd join him next year. Tommy had gone away on schedule, and Zach swallowed every pill in our house.

It had been nearly five months since Zach died, the lazy summer day was unusually hot and humid. Claire had gone to Allentown with her mom, Eric was home writing a song, and I was left to my own devices. Mother's newfound friendship with a bottle made her even more impossible to be around, giving me a good reason to get out of the house. I headed into the woods, knowing in advance the source of my destination—the tree fort.

I hadn't expected to find Tommy there, didn't even know he was back in town for the summer. He was sitting cross-legged with his back against one of the haphazardly placed pieces of plywood. I don't think he heard my approach; if he had, I'm sure he'd have removed all traces of the tears that rolled down his cheeks.

Clearing my throat, I pulled myself up through the hole in the floor. "When did you get back in town?"

Tommy's rich blue eyes swam with tears that he didn't even bother to hide. He shrugged his shoulders, snuffed, and leaned his head back against the plywood. "Been back about three weeks. I'm working with my dad."

I nodded, realizing that with Zach gone, there wasn't any reason for Tommy to come by the house.

"I-I've saved back some of Zach's things." Don't cry, I ordered myself. "She, Mother, went through and packed most of it up and had it burned." I gulped back the strangled cry that usually came with this confession. I could see my mother in a drunken rage, tearing through Zach's room, ripping down his posters and throwing his books and other belongings into a heap on the floor. Afterward, she'd sat with a pair of scissors cutting things up, his clothes, pictures, anything she could get her hands on. I'd been so shocked and terrified by her actions that I'd called my father and urged him to come home before she hurt herself.

By the time Daddy arrived, Mother had gone through a fifth of scotch and was passed out on the floor in Zach's room. Without a word, Daddy carried her to their room and put her to bed. While he tended to her, I searched through the debris, looking for mementos for Tommy and me. I hadn't found much.

I'd written Tommy, telling him of the incident and swearing him to secrecy. No one was supposed to know that Mother had been regularly crawling inside a bottle, missing work, and refusing to see everyone. Ellen Randolph's illness had been of great concern at church, just as my father's continued absence had been. I'd been gently questioned, consoled, and shown the love of God and community—until I walked through the doors at home.

Tommy held up what was left of his and Zach's old sledding trophy. Mother had done her best to destroy it, knocking the little sled from its post, and scratching at the engraving until it was nearly obliterated. It had been the only acknowledgement that she'd known where Zach's problems started. If only she'd made the connection before it was too late.

"I figured you left it here," Tommy was saying. "For all the good times it brings to mind, I can't help remembering…"

I nodded. "Did you know," I whispered. "Did you know that Davy asked for a ride?"

Tommy swallowed hard but didn't answer.

"Why couldn't Zach get it, Tommy? Why couldn't he see he wasn't to blame for what happened?"

"He got lost, Jess." He shook his head. "Then, for some reason we're never going to understand, he couldn't break free of the memory. He didn't know how to leave it in the past or deal with it in the present. I don't know, Jessie, but you can't allow yourself to follow his lead this time." Tommy Lofgren reached out and took my hand. "You always looked up to him, we all did. He was a great guy, a good brother and friend. But he was sick, Jessie, and what he did has nothing to do with you. You've got to see that. *You are not to blame.*"

How many times had I said those exact words to Zach? How many times had he appeared to listen? I know at least four times they hadn't sunk in enough to make a difference. That last and final time, that memory, hurt the most.

"If only I'd stayed home that day," I started, tears streaming down my face.

"He'd have just put it off till later, Jessie. You know that. You have to accept it, get past it. Don't let this mess claim another victim." Tommy hefted the trophy angrily, stood, strode over to the makeshift window, and threw the thing into the forest. "God never blamed anyone for Davy Brown's death, least of all

Zach. But the fool couldn't get that through his thick skull. But I'll be damned if I'm going to let you pick up where Zach left off. It's over, Jessica, do you hear me? It's over!"

~~~

I awoke to silence and a fire that was smoldering in the hearth. I'd gone through more than half of my branches the day before and then used a lot of the smaller pieces to repair cracks in the cabin's walls and floors. We needed wood for the fire, and I wasn't yet prepared to break up the furniture to satisfy that need. But going outside, having to face the havoc wrought the night before, didn't thrill me either.

Domino ran to the door in anticipation of our morning outing, but I was reluctant to allow her out before I saw what was there. I shooed her back from the door, and with a firm grip on the skillet, stepped onto the porch, pulling the door shut behind me.

The wind whipped at the ends of my scarf, tossing them into my face as it skittered by. I looked out across the snow that was no longer a pristine white. Dark stains dotted the frozen landscape just a few yards from the porch, stains of a muddy brown color. Blood.

Since it was in the path to the stand of trees where I collected the downed branches, I had no choice but to check it out. I steeled myself for what I might see, keeping alert for the slightest sound or feeling that I wasn't alone.

One of the animals had been ripped to shreds, blood, fur, and body parts spread throughout the killing field. I didn't recognize any tracks but those of the dogs. A bear would have left large prints, and would
~~~

likely have eaten the dog, but the bears were hibernating this time of year. What else? I'd thought it might be a mountain lion, but now I had to wonder. What else could have been strong enough, daring enough, to have committed such an atrocity?

I tore my eyes from the scene, forced back the bile, and continued to the edge of the woods. It became increasingly difficult to pass by the area, and finally, after the third trip, I knew what I had to do.

I returned to the site of the massacre with the kettle, then scooped up the surrounding snow and tossed it over the mutilated animal until it was completely covered. Only then did I continue with my work. Whatever killed the dog could come back at any time, and I didn't want to take any chances. I determined to get in as much wood as possible, before allowing Domino a quick, supervised run while I filled everything I could with snow to melt, then we'd barricade ourselves in the cabin for the rest of the day.

By the time we were tucked inside, it was already mid-afternoon. I was hot and sweaty from all the exertion, and while I cooked our meal, I peeled off my coat and hung it on the rocker. How I wanted to get out of these clothes! But as much as I wanted to strip and be clean, I knew it was unwise. I settled for taking an end of my scarf, wetting it, then wiping myself down.

After we ate, I used a small amount of water to rinse out the skillet rather than take it outside. I wandered about the cabin, trying to figure out other ways to keep us safe, and wondering what we would do when we finished the last of our meat. There were still a couple of granola bars and Domino's treats, but that wasn't enough to keep us going.

Late in the afternoon, my throat and ears became scratchy, and I broke out the Tylenol in an effort to counteract the oncoming cold. By evening, I was sure I had a fever. As I shrugged back into my parka, fed the fire, then huddled onto the mattress, I couldn't help wondering just how much longer we could last. Closing my eyes against the pain in my head, I surrendered to the will of God.

Chapter 39

Tommy wasn't the only one who determined I wouldn't fall into the same trap as my brother, taking on blame for something that was beyond our control. As the years wore on, my father hid more in his work, staying away long hours that incorporated participation in a bowling league, attending meetings at the Moose Lodge, and anything that kept him too busy to think. Mother, always so self-sufficient and independent, sank further into an alcoholic haze until Granny Ed stepped in. After informing Daddy of her intentions, Granny Ed packed a bag for Mother and whisked her off to Denver to dry out. I'm not sure Daddy completely understood what was going on, he was in his own little world of denial, but my grandmother made certain I knew the score. Before they left, she made arrangements with the Benton's to take me in, then off they went.

Claire's parents were awesome. It had been years since I'd been privileged to be a part of a real family, not the broken, dysfunctional one we'd become. With their help, I began to put my life into perspective. Church was good that way, too. The entire congregation at Faith Community enfolded me in their loving arms, reassuring me that I'd done all I could to help my brother. I was just starting to believe it when Eric presented me with "The Plan."

"If I stick around here and continue working with my dad, I'll get nowhere fast," he said, tossing a rock into Dover Creek where we were picnicking. "I intend to make something of my music, Jess, to *be* someone."

"What about school? I thought you'd decided to get your degree first."

"Why study music when I can play it?" He turned away from me, walked to the edge of the creek, knelt down, and began singing, *"Can't you see that earthly love and earthly faces, only give what men can give. But heavenly love and heavenly faces, show us how we're meant to live."*

The lyrics stabbed at my soul, wrenching my heart in two.

"God doesn't want you to give up earthly love, Eric." I cried. "He put us here to love one another."

"For most people, that's true." Eric took me by the shoulders and stared deeply into my eyes. "But I need to give myself totally over to Him, to write *His* songs. I have to stop thinking about what I want. If I don't concentrate on the bigger picture, I'm not going to fulfill my promise. You've got to see that, Jess. You, above everyone else, have to understand."

But I didn't, and nothing he said could change things.

Eric drove me back to Claire's, waved goodbye

and walked out of my life. By the time Granny Ed brought Mother back home, dried out, but mean and bitter, I was already set up to accept the blame in Zach's suicide. Not a single day passed without me knowing how much she'd have preferred it to have been me who died instead of Zach. I tried everything, did everything I could in the hope of changing her mind. I became more obedient, made better grades, and was quick to pick up the slack wherever it was lacking. When Mother introduced me to Jonathan Keller, I was primed and ready to accept anything that would please her. And, for a while, it looked like Jonathan filled the bill.

For his part, Jonathan seemed the perfect choice. He was handsome, ambitious, kind, sincere, and my parents loved him. What could be better?

I hadn't seen it coming, the verbal abuse that grew to include physical abuse as well. When Jonathan showed his true colors, I was already lost, trapped in a relationship with no way out. Gradually, I'd come to look at it as my just punishment for allowing my brother to die. It wasn't until I lost the baby and Daddy decided it was time to end our family tragedy that I realized God had not ordained what my life had become. With that first appointment to see Matt Harris, my father had given me a way to get back on the right track. Matt Harris, Claire, even Eric had shown me that in order to move on, I had to face the past. And in facing the past, I had to look death in the eye and win.

~~~

I pulled the blanket over my head and wished Jonathan would get up to find out who was pounding on
~~~

our door. But no, he wouldn't allow me the luxury of sleeping in, I'd have to answer the door myself if I wanted any peace.

Well, if he could ignore it, then so could I!

I put my arms over my ears in an attempt to blot out the incessant knocking. I couldn't understand why anyone would be so persistent when there was obviously no one coming.

I was fully conscious now, and the noise I thought was just part of a dream was reality.

"Open up!" A voice spoke from beyond the cabin door. "Are you all right in there?"

"Yes, yes! Just a minute." I shouted, arousing Domino enough to start her barking.

I ran to the door, unbolted it, and throwing it open, found four people in ski attire. The patches on their sleeves read "Ski Patrol, King's Mountain Resort." I figured they must have joined a State Patrol rescue party. What I couldn't fathom was how I'd managed to get so far off course. The resort was north of Allentown by quite a few miles.

I stood back to let them in. "You'll never know how glad I am to see you!"

Domino was ecstatic. Her tail wagged so fast and hard I thought it a miracle she didn't flop to and fro with it.

"Are you all right, ma'am?" This voice was softer and much higher pitched than the first one. Upon removal of the ski mask, I saw the owner was a very striking young woman.

"Ma'am?" She said again.

"Sorry. It's been so long since I've heard anyone's voice but my own that I, uh—I'm fine." I told her.

"Especially now you're here."

The others in the party followed suit, each removing his mask and questioning me about our well-being.

"Before we report in," this was the person I'd heard first, the man with the deep, resonate voice. "Ma'am? Are you listening?" He gently shook me.

Gazing into his face, I discovered he had the darkest brown eyes I'd ever seen. His almost black hair waved naturally away from his face, which showed a tenderness and concern for me that made me blush.

"I'm sorry. Please, what did you say?"

"Your name. I'd like to call in your name." He spoke loudly and very slowly as if he thought I was deaf.

"Jessica Keller. And that," I said, pointing at my dog, "is Domino."

"I'll be back with you in a moment." He went off in a corner of the cabin and spoke into his radio.

"You're a very lucky lady." One of the other men remarked.

"I beg your pardon?" I was so thrilled to have finally been discovered that I was having trouble focusing.

"If it hadn't been for the smoke from your fire, we'd never have found you."

"Oh?"

"What he means is," the girl patted Domino once more than stood and stretched. "We never thought about anyone getting this far from the highway. We wouldn't have thought to check this old cabin if Adam hadn't spotted the smoke last evening. Instead of giving up the search, we left the resort at first light. The moment Adam spotted the smoke again, he knew exactly where to come."

"I'm grateful to him—to all of you! I couldn't have held out much longer."

"And you've been up here since?" The last man asked as he fed Domino something resembling beef jerky.

"Um, four days, I think. Since the snowstorm Saturday evening."

"Wow!" They all seemed to say in unison.

I looked from one to the other of them, trying to comprehend the looks on their faces. I shook my head, the headache and sore throat from the night before suddenly taking its rightful place as top tormenter of my exhausted body. I collapsed onto the rocker in the middle of a coughing spree.

"You poor thing! Would you like something to eat? Some tea or coffee?" The girl patted my arm then felt my face and forehead. "You've got a bit of a fever, dear. We have some aspirin." She dug into her backpack.

"That's okay. I've got some Tylenol around here somewhere." I told her. "But I'd love some tea. I can't wait to drink something other than snow water. I'm not really very hungry right now, though. Guess I'm too excited to eat."

"Four days without food-"

"I didn't say that." They all turned to stare at me. "You see, Granny Ed made sure I had granola bars, and before I left, I packed food for Domino. Then, of course, there was this rabbit-" I told them all about the rabbit, how I'd been eating on it the last two days. I also told them about the wild dogs and how I'd fought them off twice, before something more dangerous attacked them. The three of them stood around me, listening intently and staring in astonishment.

"A little bitty thing like you? Who'd have thought?" Said one of the men, scratching his balding head.

"Amazing, truly amazing!"

"There was no other choice if Domino and I were to survive."

"It's okay, Ms. Keller." The girl held my arm gently. "You did great, you know?" Her face turned grim. "We've helped carry five people out of these mountains that didn't survive. So, you see, you deserve kudos."

The man they'd called Adam called the others into a conference, leaving me with my thoughts. Five people had perished! How could I, with my background, have been the one to survive?

Adam left the group and joined me.

"Can you ski?"

"I'm afraid not. Is that a problem?"

"Only if you were hoping to get home today. They can't get the snowmobile up here till tomorrow," he explained. "I'm going to send the others home, but I'll stay with you. I've got supplies, and we'll have a good meal later on. Any objections?"

On any other occasion I would have protested being left alone with a stranger, especially a man. Right now, however, the very prospect of having company, of not being alone, took precedence.

"Of course not. If I can't get down today, I can't get down. And I'll be glad for your company. After all these days with only Domino to talk to, it'll be a nice change."

"It's settled then." He said, waving the others on. They nodded at him, collected their gear, and after congratulating me again, disappeared out the door. He followed them, returning a few minutes later with a pack of supplies slung over his back.

"I failed to introduce myself. Adam Webster at your service." He held out his hand.

Taking it shyly, I smiled. "Mr. Webster. I owe you a great deal. The girl explained how you spotted the smoke from the chimney. Thank you for pursuing it." I lowered my eyes, uncomfortable with the intenseness of his gaze.

"No problem. Glad to be of service." He turned toward the fireplace, threw on some more wood, and busied himself unpacking the supplies.

I watched him, wanting to ask a question but almost afraid of hearing the answer. Instead, I showed him all the wonders of my little haven, right down to the ancient cans of beans in the bottom of the hutch.

"I knew this place was up here, had heard that hunters used it from time to time. But that was back when I was a kid. I didn't know if it still existed, to be honest with you. And I've gotta tell you, it's a real booger to try to find. If it hadn't been for the smoke…"

"That's what your partners said. I don't get it, though." I stared into the fire for a moment and then back at him. "When I left my car, I headed downhill in what I was positive was a southerly direction." I shook my head, confused. "I'm sure I headed south."

"It's understandable you got turned around, disoriented. The important thing is that you found the cabin and were able to stay out of the cold."

I nodded, agreeing with only part of his assessment. "I don't know if you believe in God, but I do—strongly. When I started out Sunday morning, it was because I felt like I was being prompted, that it was the right thing to do." I stared intently at Adam Webster, wanting to share my story, something so unlike me. "I had a lot of doubts about my ability to get through this, but I knew His strength was there for me to draw upon. All I needed was to reach out."

"And did you?"

"Not always. I fought it." I glanced away. "I don't know why we do that, fight when all He wants is to show us the way."

"Human nature, free choice. But you made it. You survived." He patted me on the shoulder then went back to work putting together sandwiches with thick pieces of ham. "Are you all right? You look a little pale."

He led me over to the rocker and helped me sit. He returned to where he'd set his pack, returning a moment later with aspirin and a bottle of water.

"These will be good for that fever."

"I'm fine. Really." Still, I took the bottles, knowing he was right about the aspirin. I shook out a couple then handed the bottle back to him. "Thanks."

"So, are you going to tell me how a nice girl like you came to be in a mess like this?"

"It wasn't easy," I laughed. "Believe me!"

"Must've been something pretty important to make you go out in that storm."

"It seemed so at the time. Besides, it didn't start snowing until I'd already started up the mountain. It was so light, I didn't believe there would be a problem making it to Allentown before it really cut loose. I miscalculated."

"So I see." We both laughed so hard Domino joined in with a high-pitched howl.

"When—when you reported finding me, were there any, I mean, had anyone reported me missing?"

"Oh, yeah, sorry. I meant to tell you. Your parents, grandmother, and your friend, Matt Harris, have all been insisting you were somewhere on the mountain. And from what I understand, your grandmother was relentless." He smiled. "You have quite a support group there."

All of them. Incredible!

I smiled, leaning back into the rocker. Matt Harris, the therapist Daddy insisted I see, the guy I'd been dancing around, who I'd avoided telling what was really going on in my life.

As darkness fell, our conversation lulled, and a peaceful silence descended over the cabin. We ate the ham sandwiches, drank plenty of bottled water, and enjoyed the crackling warmth of the fire.

"Well, we'd better get some sleep. They'll be here first thing in the morning to get us down to the resort." He stood up, grabbed his flashlight, and headed for the door. "I'll be back in a moment."

I'd been used to having to use the porcelain bowl as my bathroom and had been wondering what to do with him there. Once he left, I hurried to my corner and relieved myself in haste. I was pulling my clothes back into place when Adam flew back inside the cabin, his clothes askew, his eyes wide.

"Are the dogs back?" I rushed toward the door and bolted it as he straightened his clothing.

"No, worse. A wolverine." As he sank onto the

rocker, I saw that his hands were shaking. "When you told me the story about something attacking those dogs, I was thinking more along the line of a mountain lion. But a wolverine-"

Strange clicking noises sounded on the small porch, and I moved away from the door, ready to grab a weapon to defend myself.

"It's okay, Jessica. I've got a pistol in my pack, but I don't think we'll need it."

I didn't want to take any chances. I got the pack and handed it to him.

"If it's all right with you, I'm going to sit this one out."

Chapter 40

Zach sat on the edge of the mattress watching me. I wondered how long he'd been there and was a little perturbed he'd come in so early and awakened me.

"Hi, Jess." He grinned like he always did at these times, bashful and a little ashamed of giving me a start.

"What's up?" I rubbed my eyes and tried to sit, but for some reason, seemed unable to move.

Zach put a hand on my leg and rubbed it reassuringly. "Don't worry, kiddo. You're fine. Just a little stiff."

He moved closer, his grin widening into a smile. "You know how proud I am of you, Jessie-girl? You've shown us all what you're made of, and that's the greatest gift you could ever give me."

"I don't understand." Again, I tried to move and found it impossible. "Zach, what's wrong with me, what's happened?"

"Shush, now, Jessie. I've only got a moment." He

touched my forehead, my cheek, rubbing it like he had when I was little and he was trying to soothe me. "I never meant for you to blame yourself, sis. I never meant for my illness to touch you—or mom and dad. I know why it did, but it's not what I wanted. I just wasn't thinking straight. But you, you've got your whole life ahead of you now, Jessie. You can break free of the past and Jonathan. Build a real life for yourself."

"Jonathan?" How did he know about Jonathan? I didn't meet him until *after* Zach died.

Sudden tears of realization stung my eyes. I reached toward my brother wanting to touch him, to hold him—to finally have the chance to say goodbye.

"It's okay, Jessie. *You're* okay."

I felt the feather light touch on my cheek again and leaned into his hand.

"Trust God, sis, just like you've done these last four days. He's got a plan for you. Talk to Claire and Tommy, they know I'm right. So does Dr. Harris. I like him. He's good for you."

I awoke to the delicious fragrance of bacon and eggs. I frantically searched the corners of the cabin, hoping Zach still lingered there. Could it really have been a dream? It had felt so real.

"Morning." Adam smiled. "Hope you're hungry 'cause breakfast's about ready."

"Great, I'm starved." I stood up and stretched. "What time is it? My watch seems to have died."

"Around seven. We have about an hour until the snowmobile is here."

We ate in silence, Adam eyeing me quizzically when he wasn't tossing food down to Domino. As much as I wanted to share my dream, to talk about what it might mean, Adam Webster wasn't the man I wanted to speak to about it.

That man was down in Bennington.

Precisely at eight, we heard the unmistakable drone of snowmobiles coming toward the cabin. I gathered the rest of my belongings and prepared for departure.

"You about ready?"

I nodded, taking a final look around the cabin. I was about to follow him out the door when I remembered the love beads.

"There's one more thing I have to do," I told him.

"Okay. I'll load your stuff." He picked up the picnic hamper—minus Domino—smiled, and went out the door.

I carefully removed the necklace, located the newspaper the beads had originally been in, rewrapped them, and placed the package on a shelf inside the hutch.

"Thanks for your ray of hope, Sunshine. Maybe they'll help remind the next person who comes here that God's there for them, too." I patted my chest and held out my arms to Domino. She jumped up, and I held her tightly.

"Let's go start our new life, Dom."

I walked out into the warm sunshine, my boots crunching the snow as I made my way to the snowmobile.

Adam introduced me to the driver, then helped me aboard.

"Hope to see you again, Jessie," he said with a smile.

I took his hand and squeezed it. "Thanks, Adam. I'll never forget you."

"Hold on tight." He told me as he motioned for the driver to go.

As much as I wanted to turn around, I didn't. I'd spent enough of my life looking at what had gone before and wasn't going to spend the future that way. I'd get a divorce from Jonathan, get the therapy I needed to get past all the abuse I'd suffered at his hands, and move on from there. I didn't know what the future held for me. I didn't have to know. All I had to do was continue listening to that still small voice that led me to the cabin in the middle of nowhere.

Or maybe that cabin was right where it was supposed to be, just this side of heaven.

THE END

NATIONAL SUICIDE PREVENTION LIFELINE: 1-800-273-8255
NATIONAL DOMESTIC VIOLENCE HOTLINE: 1-800-799-7233
OTHER BOOKS BY ALICE K. ARENZ

Hiding From Christmas
Fun, Light Romance with humor

No matter how hard she tries, Maddie Kelley can't seem to fit in at Ornamental, a company founded by her great grandfather and his best friend. Now, after yet another screw-up, she's been sent into the "enemy's" camp—two hours away from home for the next two months.

A punishment or a blessing?

Her life is turned upside down when the mundane turns unexpected, and she finally discovers where her heart truly lies.

This is the fourth novel set in the fictional Missouri community of Tarryton. Come visit old friends and make some new ones!

https://www.amazon.com/gp/product/B07XMS85DW/ref=dbs_a_def_rwt_hsch_vapi_tkin_p1_i0

Dark of Night
Where Nightmares Become Reality
Romantic Suspense

Determined to get justice for the brutal murders of her parents twenty years ago, Kelsey Carol returns to the scene of the crime—Seaton, Missouri. But what she quickly learns is that every clue brings more questions than answers. And nightmares really do come true.

The Wedding Barter
Romance

Riley Carr has been best friends with Amy Lawton since they were toddlers. While Amy awaits her discharge from the Army, Riley's been left in charge of helping to arrange "a very small, intimate ceremony with no fanfare" for Amy and her fiancé. But Riley has something else in mind.

With the aid of two other friends, Riley presents her "wedding barter" idea to groom, David Herron. He agrees, providing best man, Mike Todd, stays in the loop to keep things from getting out of hand.

It doesn't help that the giant of a man is threatening, overbearing, and just doesn't seem to like her or her ideas. But, when Todd gives Riley an ultimatum of producing results in three weeks or he'll take over, she's determined to prove him wrong. . .in more ways than one.

Portrait of Jenny
Romantic Suspense

Not even a beautiful woman can save Richard Tanner from his past.

Following an explosive—and public—argument with his ex-girlfriend, artist Richard Tanner races into a rainstorm, gripped by a powerful migraine. He wanders to the gazebo in University Park, where he meets the beautiful and mysterious Jenny—a brief encounter that leaves an indelible impression on his mind—and in his paintings.

When Detective Jack Hargrave accuses Richard of the brutal assault on his ex, he finds himself confronting demons of a past he doesn't remember. A time when little Richie Tanner walked into University Park whole, was beaten and left to die…a time that may hold the key to his future.

https://www.amazon.com/Portrait-Jenny-Alice-K-Arenz-ebook/dp/B01ESLPL1Y

An American Gothic
Mystery/Romantic Suspense/Gothic

She came to Foxxemoor to write a mystery, not to become part of one.

Devastated by the death of a child in her care, Lyssie's heart strings are tugged when she finds another child in danger. Amid past secrets, lies, and betrayals of an old college friend's family, she must choose a twin brother to trust. If she makes the wrong decision, she could not only lose her own life, but also the life of the child she's come to love.

https://www.amazon.com/gp/product/B013J4599K/ref=dbs_a_def_rwt_hsch_vapi_tkin_p1_i5

The Case of the Bouncing Grandma
Book 1 – The Bouncing Grandma Mysteries
Cozy Mystery

Has Glory hit her head one too many times, or was there really a foot dangling out of that carpet?

Reduced to watching new neighbors move in as a form of amusement, Glory Harper is stuck in a wheelchair with a broken leg, bored, and itching for some excitement. She just doesn't expect it to come in the form of a foot dangling out the back of a carpet as it's carried into her new neighbor's house. The problem is getting someone to believe her.

The moment police recognize Glory as the woman whose misadventures have given her a sketchy reputation, her believability quotient lowers considerably. Just when she thinks someone's taking her seriously, Glory realizes Detective Rick Spencer, a Harrison Ford look alike, appears more interested in her than in her story.

But, while she's looking in what seems the obvious direction to solve this mystery, the real criminals are hot on her trail.

https://www.amazon.com/gp/product/B014V1Q8R2/ref=dbs _a_def_rwt_hsch_vapi_tkin_p2_i1

The Case of the Mystified M.D.
Book 2 – The Bouncing Grandma Mysteries
Cozy Mystery

First a foot, now a hand—what body part is next?

When her puppy finds a severed hand on a walking trail, Glory Harper is positive the signet ring belongs to a missing college professor who caused a lot of trouble around town before his disappearance. Her insatiable desire to solve the mystery of his murder finds her in over her head with a community filled with secrets, blackmail, and arson.

With her sister Jane overwhelmed by trouble with her

fiancé and an arson fire in her home, Glory latches onto an unlikely partner, and soon feels as though she's stepped into an episode of the *Twilight Zone*—where nothing is as it appears, and danger lurks around every corner . . .

Including from her boyfriend, Detective Rick Spencer.

https://www.amazon.com/gp/product/B01577WKQ2/ref=series_rw_dp_sw

Mirrored Image
Classic Romantic Suspense

Their faces were the same, will their fates be as well?
Eccentric newspaper columnist Cassandra Chase and by-the-book Detective Jeff McMichaels clash over the murder investigation of Lynette Sandler—a woman who looks eerily like the popular columnist.

For McMichaels, the Sandler case becomes more than a test of his mental acumen. Despite departmental regulations and his own common sense, he finds himself drawn to a woman he was determined to dislike. While he and the department are hunting a murderer, Cassie sees the uncanny similarities between her and Lynette's lives as a reason to launch her own investigation—and what she uncovers gives her the sneaking suspicion that she, not Lynette Sandler, was the murderer's original mark.

She just needs to stay alive long enough to prove it.

https://www.amazon.com/Mirrored-Image-Alice-K-Arenz-ebook/dp/B015RKO4OU

SHORT STORY
Mystery
Home Cookin'

The new, beautiful little subdivision of Serenity View isn't all it's cracked up to be—unless you're talking about the sheetrock, driveways, or foundations of the houses! There's more hidden behind the walls in these houses than skeletons in the proverbial closet. But home builder and contractor Bubba Payton has met his match. And when he's found dead in his prized pecan grove, there are more than enough suspects…maybe even the crows that live in the grove!

https://www.amazon.com/gp/product/B01K8PQXKM/ref=dbs_a_def_rwt_hsch_vapi_tkin_p1_i11

ABOUT THE AUTHOR

Mysteries, Cozy Mysteries, Suspense, Romance, and Women's Fiction--writing across the spectrum with a Pinch of Humor and a Twist of Faith.

Alice K. Arenz has been writing since she was a child. Her earliest publications were in the small, family-owned newspaper where her articles, essays, and poems were frequently included. A member of American Christian Fiction Writers, Arenz is a Carol Award winner and two-time finalist. She writes "clean" fiction as well as Christian fiction in a variety of genres and lengths.

Follow Alice at: https://www.amazon.com/Alice-K-Arenz/e/B004DTBXL4

BookBub: https://www.bookbub.com/authors/alice-k-arenz
Goodreads: https://www.goodreads.com/author/show/3408650.Alice_K_Arenz